I'LL KNOW ME WHEN I FIND ME

I'LL KNOW ME WHEN I FIND ME

HELEN J. DARLING

BRICOLAGE
BOOKS

Cover illustration by Cécile Metzger, https://oocoucou.blogspot.com/. Instagram: @coucou_illustration

Cover design by Asya Blue, http://asyablue.com/

Printed in the United States of America

First Printing, 2018

This is a work of fiction. Names, characters, places, and incidents are products of the author's imagination or are used fictitiously. Digital profiles such as Thea's LinkedIn profile did not exist in actuality at the time of publication and reasonable efforts were made to avoid confusion with any real person. Any resemblance to actual persons living or dead, or to businesses, companies, events, or locales is purely coincidental and wholly unintended by the author. Neither the author nor the publisher is responsible for websites (or their contents) that are not owned by the author or publisher.

ISBN-13 978-0-9997003-0-3

Library of Congress Control Number: 2018930655

Bricolage Books

PO Box 52063

Durham, NC 27717-2063

www.bricolagebooks.com

I love my family dearly,
but this book is for me.

"Go confidently in the direction of your dreams. Live the life you have imagined."

Henry David Thoreau (paraphrase)

"If you don't know where you are going, you'll end up someplace else."

Yogi Berra

CHAPTER ONE

I was operating on "Jane time," which runs roughly twenty minutes later than everyone else's, but of course Thea expected that. And if I knew Thea, by the time I arrived at the restaurant she'd have a table for us, and she'd probably have ordered my seltzer for me, or something she knows I'll like even better.

Thea's the one who turned me on to seltzer instead of soft drinks and yoga pants instead of sweats, not to mention every Netflix series I watch. Whether it's because we've known each other since we were kids, or because she's just savvy that way, her instincts are spot-on. If she weren't my best friend I'd find it spooky, but since she is, it's great. It's like having a shortcut to a fabulous life.

I left work on time to meet her, a historical first, but I stopped to check on Sam, the homeless guy who resides in the doorway of the corner bank. I met him and his labrador mix, Pete, two years ago when he asked me for some change. He'd seen me come out of Walgreens with a fistful of cash, so I couldn't say no; we chatted about Pete, and now I stop to check on them a few times a week. They're both sweethearts. Sam won't let me take him to the VA, but he lets me take Pete to the veterinarian. I like to pretend I'm saving the world, one soul at a time.

The restaurant where I was meeting Thea was three blocks away, exactly halfway between my office and hers. Given that it was June in DC, it was so humid that my glasses had fogged up the second I walked out the revolving door of my building. Half a block after I visited Sam, I knew I'd need the change of clothes I kept under my desk. It was definitely a two-outfit day.

Lunch with Thea had been our Friday ritual for a few years now. We both looked forward to it, as if we were kicking off the weekend early, and like any office stiff, I'm always glad to get the weekend started. I mean, I like my job. It wasn't what I envisioned doing when I graduated from college, but that was ten years ago (okay, thirteen). You have to make choices. Being an editor of a trade magazine in DC might have a low glamor quotient, but it ranks high on the list of Jobs You Don't Take Home with You at Night.

Another thing I wouldn't be taking home with me tonight: my pantyhose, which, I noticed in the window of a corner deli, had a rip in them. That's me: always polished (with saliva) and put together (with duct tape). I didn't have a change of hosiery under my desk, so I'd pop into Walgreens to pick up a pair on my way back. The torn stockings weren't the end of my bedraggled appearance, but I put it out of my mind for the time being. My best friend didn't care that I brought my B Game when it came to personal style.

When I was a few doors away, I spied Thea sitting in the restaurant window seat. Her back was toward me, but I could tell it was her. She has this way of holding her head up very straight with her chin held high, as if she's balancing an imaginary book on her head. I should copy her posture. My mom tells me I'm going to have a hump-back when I'm old. I love how she still nags me to sit up straight.

Our friend Narin was also in the restaurant. Sometimes she joined us for Friday lunches, sometimes not; she's a lawyer and perpetually swamped with work. As I drew closer, I could tell from her posture that something was up. She leaned over the table and held Thea's hands. Maybe Richard finally asked Thea to move in with him? That'd be awkward, since Thea just closed on her house, and Richard was obsessed with his loft apartment. I thought Thea should dump Richard and move on, but I hadn't figured out how to drop this hint to her.

"Hi, ladies!" I said as I walked up to the table. "Happy Friday!"

But the minute I sat down and looked at Thea's face, I could tell Richard hadn't asked her to move in.

"What's the matter, sweetie?" I asked.

Thea's eyes were closed. She was fighting to keep it together in a public place.

"Do you want me to move us to a booth? Where it's more private?" Believe me, for Thea nothing could be worse than to break down sobbing in a restaurant with a roomful of strangers watching. "Excuse me, miss?" I said to a passing waitress. "Could you move us to a booth, please? One in the back?"

"It's not necessary," Thea said, shaking her head, her eyes still closed.

The waitress looked at me, but I nodded. "We need a booth," I whispered.

She glanced around and shrugged. "I'll see what's available."

The place was packed, but soon the waitress waved at me near the door to the kitchen.

"Come on," I said to Thea and Narin. "She's got us a booth, where we'll have some privacy." I picked up Thea's purse for her. "Narin, can you carry her drink?"

"Look, it's not necessary," Thea said, but her voice quivered.

The waitress glared at me, with her hands on her hips. A pack of hungry Hill types, new college grads in their interview suits who think they're super important because they work on Capitol Hill, hovered around the waitress, trying to maneuver into our booth.

"Let's go. People are going to take our booth." I pulled Thea to her feet and led her through the crowded tables. Narin brought up the rear with drinks in both hands.

"Thanks," I told the waitress. To the college boys in their interview suits, I said, "Take our table by the window."

"Now," I said, turning to Thea, who tucked into the booth facing away from the other diners. "What's the matter? What's happened?"

Her chin still held high, Thea's eyes watered but didn't

spill a drop. Man, she was so dignified. I could never keep it together like her.

"I've lost my job," she said. "They've eliminated our department and are sending the jobs to a processing center overseas. They just told us. We can pick up our severance-package details after lunch, then go home."

"Oh my God!" I said, maybe a little too loudly. Thea did something with processing health-insurance claims. I've never quite understood it because it seemed like the most boring thing in the world, but Thea liked her job. And she just bought her house.

Narin slipped an arm around Thea's shoulder, giving her a hug. It was awkward because they sat side by side, but she made it work. "That's awful. You deserve so much better."

Thea rested her head on Narin's shoulder.

"That's true," I agreed. "You definitely deserve better. It's horrible that companies keep ditching good people to save a few bucks. But don't worry. You'll find a new job soon."

Thea exhaled a long ragged breath. She rested her elbows on the table—something she never does because her manners are impeccable—and covered her face with her hands.

I've only seen Thea this upset in public once before. I've known her since I was eight, and even then, she had an almost regal aura about her. She's usually so stiff-upper-lip, she's practically Queen Elizabeth.

The waitress headed for our table.

"Thea? What do you want to eat?" I asked. "The waitress is coming. I'll order for you."

"I'm not hungry," Thea said.

"Narin?"

"I'll just have a veggie wrap," she said, turning back to Thea.

I jumped up to meet the waitress before she could come to the table. Okay, it was a little weird, but I knew Thea wouldn't want anyone, not even the waitress, to see her cry.

"A veggie wrap, a club sandwich, and an extra plate of french fries," I said. Fries made everything better. Thea wouldn't say no to them.

The waitress looked at me like I'd grown a horn in the center of my head, but she took my order and left. Crisis averted.

I sat back down. Thea was telling Narin about the whole episode. "They called us all into the conference room, and we thought they were going to tell us details about the merger." Thea's company just bought a smaller company that does the same stuff. "And I guess we were right, in a way, but we didn't expect *these* details. The whole marketing department got fired, and the other company's marketing people are taking over. That never happens! And all the claims people got fired, and they're outsourcing our jobs."

Technically, it's called offshoring, but now wasn't the time to get picky about semantics.

"Unbelievable." Narin rubbed Thea's back.

"I'm in shock." Thea's face still rested in her hands, so I could barely hear her. I leaned over the table so I could make out what she said. "I mean, three months ago we were getting praise from the C-suite for all the money we'd saved the company, and we all got bonuses. They were making noise about what a great year we were going to have. God, if I'd seen this coming I'd never have bought the house."

"But you love the house," I said. "You've always wanted it. You've been dreaming about this for years."

Thea shrugged. "Maybe it's just not the time."

"It is!" I said. "Don't worry. You're going to be fine. We'll come up with a plan. Won't we, Narin? Thea, believe me," I said, reaching for her hands. "We are not going to let you lose your house."

CHAPTER TWO

O n my way back to work, I gave Sam the half of my lunch I'd asked the waitress to box up, but I was too distracted to talk. I walked right by Walgreens, forgetting that I needed another pair of panty-hose. I didn't remember anything about it until Keith, the creep who works on *Cement World*, made a crack as I walked back to my office.

"Hey, Desmond, what happened to your leg? Looks like you got clawed by an animal."

Keith thinks he's edgy and clever. If he's so clever, how come he's working at *Cement World*?

Not that I had a lot of room to talk. As the associate editor of *Recycling World*, the flagship publication of Mercatur Media and the leading source of news and analysis for the construction debris-recycling industry, I didn't spend my workday honing my skills to participate in any modern-day Algonquin Round Table. The only vicious circle I regularly saw was our editorial calendar, rotating annually from Waste Expo to ShingleFest to Brick-Fair to the C&D Winter Carnival. Before I started working here, I had no idea that shingles and concrete and scrap wood even got recycled. I assumed it all went to a landfill somewhere.

If I'm lucky, I might work my way up to be the managing editor of a suite of magazines: *Cement World, Pipe World, Recycling World* ("It's all about branding, Jane,") *Roofing Outlook,* and the start-up digital newsletter *Dust Suppression Monthly.* Or I can try and make the jump to the transportation mags: *Fleet Management, Parking Today,* and *Tires.*

Max Perkins, eat your dead heart out.

While I don't doubt that the iconic book editor would have wrestled a more inspirational narrative out of the asbestos remediation reportage that regularly lands on my desk, I've been promoted twice so I must be doing something right. Over the years, my salary has climbed from anemic to mediocre to sustainable to healthy. I'd be lying if I said the job didn't have a generous retirement plan and decent healthcare. A lot of people make the same choice: you trade work you love for rewards you've grown accustomed to. Welcome to adulthood.

I slogged through the edits on the monthly columns and started on the cover article on Waste Expo 2017. Usually I can bang right through this type of work on autopilot, but today I couldn't focus. On top of that, my stomach kept churning in a way I couldn't ignore. Since when did something as benign as a club sandwich produce indigestion? Combined with the tension that was winding my shoulders together, I felt like the crumpled-up wads of paper that moments ago I'd been tearing through with my bright red pen.

I found a couple of lint-covered antacid tablets in my purse and knocked them back with a glass of water. All I thought about was Thea. What was she doing now? Was she in a cab on her way home, a cardboard box in her lap? Was she an anxious wreck? Did she keep it together until she got home? Was she now weeping on her couch?

I picked up my phone and texted her: "Thinking of you. XOXOXOXO"

I needed to do more. This felt huge to me, unprecedented in scope in Thea's life. It was an odd feeling to have—Thea's mom dying should feel bigger, but that happened long ago, back when we were in middle school.

She'd gotten breast cancer, and by the time the doctors discovered the tumors it was way too late to help her in a meaningful way. Nevertheless, Mrs. Willis wanted to go down fighting, so she signed on for chemotherapy and radiation. She lost her hair; her skin, which she had cared for so tenderly and assiduously throughout her life, first developed a translucent, almost ashy quality, then rashlike bumps, then finally looked burnt, like toast.

"It feels crispy," she complained as Thea and I sat beside her hospital bed, rubbing lotion onto her hands and arms and legs day after day. I never contributed to the conversation on those days, except to answer politely when spoken to, and only responding to the specific questions I was asked. "How is school, dear?" "It's going well, Mrs. Willis," I'd respond, even when Thea knew I was lying to her mother's face. What else could I say? I was a kid, and compared to hers, my life was a nonstop holiday.

Mom and I took Thea to the hospital every day. Mom dropped us off, and I sat with Thea when she wanted me, and I waited down the hall when she and her mom wanted time alone.

"Do you want me to come with you?" I asked every time, assuming one day she'd say no. But she never did. "It helps not having to go in or leave by myself," she explained.

So I went in with her, and I left with her. Sometimes I sat with her and her mother, watching as Thea painted on eyebrows when her mother's fell out or applied tinted lip balm to her mother's parched and peeling lips. Sometimes I sat in the waiting room, watching the traffic out the window or reading the aged magazines scattered on the table. I lived for the moments I could run to the nurses' station and beg them for cups of ice water or juice for the two of them.

I held Thea's hand a lot those few months, in the elevator or on the bench as we waited for my mom to bring us home. I sat next to Thea on the sofa while we watched stupid movies, or at the kitchen table as we did homework. My mother, meanwhile, marshaled an army of neighbors and friends, filling the Willises' freezer with food for months and organizing people to carpool or clean their house. Every time we saw Thea's dad, he said, "Thank God for your mother, Jane. I don't know how we'd get through this without her."

I turned back to the article, but the words blurred together.

The freelancer's digital photos meant to accompany the story offered a momentary distraction but not a good one. As I clicked through them, my irritation grew. They couldn't be more useless. All the equipment photos were shot from a distance. He hadn't even taken advantage of the press day to get pictures without expo-goers wandering into the frame. The photos were neither well lit nor interesting. The best one was of three overweight, middle-aged men standing in front of a fancy conveyer-belt apparatus in the middle of a warehouse. It looked like the worst vacation snapshot ever.

I heard my mom's voice in my head. "Well, honey, if it was fun it wouldn't be called *work*."

"AAUGH!" I shouted at my screen.

My phone pinged Thea's special text alarm. I seized it and read her reply: "Thx"

Maybe it's because I work in publishing, but I can't text in shorthand, and I don't skip punctuation. It's just not right. I wrote back: "Shall I pick up some takeout and come to your place later?"

Thea: "IDK, maybe"

First the article, now the text exchange. Neither was getting anywhere. My nerves twitched until I felt like I was going to burst out of my skin. Behind the closed office door, I kicked off my heels, stripped off the shredded pantyhose, and jumped up and down in place, as quietly as I could, to burn off some of the energy. Winded, I sat down and tried again to focus, but I felt like those nights when my body wants to sleep but my mind wants to zip around like a hummingbird on speed. Pure torture. By three thirty I'd read the same paragraph five times and it still didn't make any sense, so I gave up.

"I've got to head out a little early," I said to Sarah, the intern. "Have a good weekend."

I made a point to go the long way around to the elevator, avoiding the *Cement World* cubicles. But the day being disastrous and me being me, I met Keith coming out of the men's room.

"Leaving already?" he asked, wiping his hands on his pants.

"Yeah," I said, punching the elevator button harder. Our building is an old one, and while the elevator doesn't require an attendant to raise and lower a metal safety door, it's barely more modern, and prone to failure. Like now, apparently.

"You look nice. Doing anything fun this weekend?"

Ohhh, no. I didn't look nice—I looked slovenly, and he knew it—and I didn't like where this was headed. "Yes," I said, pretending to check my phone for messages. I hoped there would be one from, say, a guardian angel, giving me brilliant, step-by-step instructions on how to shut Keith down, permanently.

He came closer. "Like what?"

"Like," I said, and froze.

Given that I get into this situation all the time, you'd think I'd be an ace at lying on the spot, but you'd be wrong. Later, on the Metro, I thought up all kinds of excuses, but when I needed them, where were they? Just floating around in the ether, unhelpfully displaced by lyrics to early-nineties pop songs.

"Like what?"

"I'm...going clubbing. With friends." The lie came courtesy of Marky Mark and the Funky Bunch, the artist currently broadcasting on my chronic mental soundtrack.

Keith's eyebrows rose like my impatience. "Is that so? I didn't know you liked to dance. Me, too. Maybe we can go sometime after work."

As if to grind home the point that I don't actually believe in guardian angels, my phone died. The elevator arrived, but its doors opened only a few inches and paused. I forced them apart with my shoulder and hip, keeping nose to dead phone screen. Of course he knew I heard him; the hallway was so deserted I wouldn't have been surprised to see tumbleweeds blowing away from *Dust Suppression Monthly*.

"What do you think?" he asked.

I punched the L button like I was trying to launch the Space Shuttle.

"We'll talk about it later. Have a good weekend!" I said, as the doors crept closed.

Why did I say that? I didn't want to talk about it later. I didn't want to talk about it *ever*.

I wasn't going clubbing because I never go clubbing. I used to tell myself I'd meet someone if I did. But when the time came to get dressed up and go out, I told myself I would probably meet someone like Keith, which gave me permission to stay home in my yoga pants and old T-shirts.

"Maybe you should go to church," my mom once suggested, like that's a hot pickup joint.

Keith is just one example of what's wrong with my personal life. If I had to describe him, I'd say things like, he's average build. Brown hair and eyes. If I showed you his photo, you'd probably think, "He's not so bad." Keith's not attractive, but he's not unattractive. He's just dull; as the saying goes, there's no *there* there. He once came into the office on a weekend wearing jeans and a T-shirt that said, "Meh." I laughed out loud when I saw it, not because I liked the shirt but because it was such a clear-cut and rare example of truth in advertising.

His creepiness derives entirely from his persistence in asking me out. To be honest, if he'd just back off I'd probably find him agreeable, if not appealing. Maybe it's me, but there's something off-putting about someone who wants you so badly. There's a dissertation in there somewhere, about the need to play flirtatious games, to pursue what we perceive to be scarce emotional commodities. We should all be evolved beyond such games by now, in my opinion. Maybe it's biological. I'll try to remember to Google that idea when I have time. If anyone's doing a study on that, I want to know the findings. They'd be more useful to my life than the articles in *Cosmo* I keep consulting.

Sometimes I wonder if I should just agree to have a drink with Keith, if that would kill the urge for him to ask me out again. (Does he think I'm playing the game when I'm really, *really* not?) But I can't agree, because (A), saying yes would feel like I was admitting "you're right, world, this is the best I can do." And (B), it would probably backfire, and he'd be all over me at work. So I continue to resist. I tell myself to be patient, good things are just around the corner. For God's sake, they have to be.

When I stepped into the lobby I realized I didn't know

what to do with myself. I continued outside to the sidewalk, where the heat hung on me like a wet towel. I couldn't stay outside for long.

An air-conditioned chain bookstore beckoned from the opposite corner. I crossed the street in front of a city bus; idling next to me, it felt like it was breathing on me (like a mechanical Keith, ugh!). Pushing him further from my mind, I dragged open the bookstore's heavy door and stepped inside.

Four floors of vast shelves rose up above the street. I consulted the directory and headed to the third floor, where the business and career books were kept.

Six whole shelves' worth of strategies to find a job stared me down, daring me to choose among them. The fact that I didn't know exactly what Thea did made it more complicated, but maybe job advice was job advice, regardless? I didn't know. I started working at *Recycling World* right out of college and hadn't gotten around to looking elsewhere.

I picked up books and started reading the back covers. Some of them promised finding your dream job, some promised finding a job in under an hour, some guaranteed you could get rich quick by being a slumlord (not in so many words). There was even a series on "How to Get a Job as a…" Game designer. Fashion model. Hedge fund manager. Blogger. Bartender. Bounty hunter? I decided to get that one, just to cheer her up.

I picked up the classic *What Color Is Your Parachute?*, which from the title you wouldn't think would be a job book but it is, and a book on how to find a job in an hour, in case she was desperate. Then I picked up some fancy interior design magazines for me and a box of Godiva chocolates at the checkout because they were there. I intended them for Thea, but if they didn't make it to her, well, it wouldn't be the first time.

The clerk ringing up my purchase said sympathetically, "Were you downsized, too? I used to be an accountant."

"It's for my friend," I said.

He nodded, and immediately I realized that he thought they were for me but I couldn't admit it.

"Her name's Thea," I said. "She used to work for Janus Insurance, but they just downsized everyone in their claims department. No, I work across the street, for Mercatur Media. Trade magazines, you know. Your one-stop shop for construction-industry business intelligence. It's not glamorous, but I figure I'm safe until the AI robots come for me."

The register displayed the total: $115.37.

Oh my God. How did that happen? Then I realized that those fancy magazines were not like the five-dollar ones I usually got at the drugstore. Sure enough, they each cost around fifteen to twenty dollars—and more for the ones from overseas (priced in euros, crap!) that showed French and Italian homes. I didn't have that kind of money to be spending it left, right, and center, but I plastered on a grin as I swiped my credit card and swore to myself I'd lock it away when I got home.

He handed me the bag. "Have a good one."

Back out on the street with my flimsy plastic bag, which

weighed a ton now that it was stuffed full of paper, I tried to figure out what came next. The book shopping killed an hour, but it was too early to get dinner to take to Thea's. I decided to go home because I didn't want to carry my briefcase with me all evening, and it was definitely time to ditch the heels.

My apartment is way out on the end of Connecticut Avenue, literally yards from the Maryland state line. I've lived there since I graduated from college. The place is tiny—too small, really—but when I think about the hassle and expense of moving, I want to burrow under my quasi-lofted bed amongst the suitcases jammed with out-of-season clothes and hide. It's such an ordeal: hiring movers, watching to make sure nobody steals your stuff out of the back of the truck, getting your services set up at the next place, telling everybody your change of address, unpacking. I mean, I've lived here ten (thirteen) years and I still have boxes I haven't unpacked. On the plus side, after living so long like I'm still in college, I'm only three installments away from paying off my student loans.

Unfortunately, my little neighborhood is several blocks from the Metro station. The handles of the plastic shopping bag from the bookstore cut into my fingers as I trudged home. I tried on the train to put the shopping bag into my briefcase, but I couldn't close it because guess who never cleans out her bag? So I passed it back and forth between my cramped hands and hoped I'd make it home before it severed my fingertips.

In my building, I extracted the contents of my mailbox and dumped them into the plastic bag. Upstairs, I spilled everything onto the kitchen table and flexed my fingers to bring the blood back to the tips.

Mostly junk: credit card offers, promotional postcards from local gyms. A new issue of *InStyle*, though, and two cards from college friends.

Alas, birth announcements, both of them. Welcome to the world, little Lucy, 6 lb. 4 oz., 18 inches long, and Noah, 7 lb. 9 oz., 19 inches long. Sleek matte-finished cards displayed collaged pictures of tiny fists and feet, plus adorable graphics of elephants and lions and birds. Lucy's whole-body photo showed her bound up like a burrito, her mouth open in a perfect, tiny *O*, dark eyes staring at the camera with suspicion.

My mother would gladly sell a kidney to be able to send out cards like these. Unfortunately for her—and worse for me—I don't have any siblings to pick up my slack.

My blouse still clung to me, and now that I had returned to a hospitable environment, my sweaty skin felt clammy. I slipped out of my work clothes and took a shower. As I dried my hair, I flipped through the new *InStyle*.

Why do I continue to subscribe to this magazine when I never take its suggestions? Every issue tells me what a thirty-something woman should wear, but I prefer the look they recommend for age fifty-plus. Fifty-plus women are serious about their comfort, as am I. Dressing like a grandmother may be directly correlated to my lackluster dating life, but when I let Thea or another friend style me, I feel like a fraud.

"You've got to get serious. Dress your age," my friend

Brooke said to me in December—the last time I let her "help" me. Brooke and I lived together for a disastrous year when I first moved to DC. Her declared major was psychology, and while such a course of study could have prepared her for a lifetime of useful service to humanity, she'd applied her studies to a dogged pursuit of her Mrs. degree. Now engaged to a tobacco lobbyist making seven figures a year, she needed a new project. So at New Year's I let her play Pygmalion.

She'd unbuttoned another button on my blouse and stepped back to consider her work. "Are those the sexiest shoes you have?" she asked, eyeing my plain black 1 ½-inch heels. "I've got to take you shopping. We'll go to Saks. I'll even treat you."

"You don't have to do that."

"It's my favorite kind of community service!" She giggled. "And there's a fabulous day spa out near Tysons. Oh, your poor cuticles." She shook her head, giving my hands a sympathetic smile.

"I'm good," I said, stepping out of the heels and buttoning my shirt up to the top.

"Sweetie, I'm telling you this because I know if it were the other way around, I'd want you to tell me." She laid two elegantly manicured hands on my elbows and looked me in the eye. "You can't go to a club looking like the retirement home activity bus just dropped you off. You're never going to get a man if you dress like that."

"I'd prefer a guy who doesn't care about my cleavage," I said.

Brooke dropped her hands from my arms and picked up her Prada bag and Chanel overcoat. Then she shook her head at me, glossy locks brushing her shoulders. "Honey, those don't exist." She looked me up and down. "When you're ready to take your dating life seriously, you know who to call. Steven's got tons of associates with cash to burn if you're willing to work on yourself a little."

CHAPTER THREE

Babies? Brooke? Bah.

I didn't want to play games. Call me idealistic, but I didn't think wanting a relationship based on something more substantial than a push-up bra was asking for too much. Although the available evidence pointed to the contrary, I believed that someone existed who knew beauty might be more than exposed-skin deep. Until that person materialized, forget it. I was a modern woman. I didn't need any of it.

I threw the *InStyle* on the corner chair and pulled on shorts and a grubby T-shirt from college that, after probably a thousand washings, now had the texture of fine silk. I put my wet hair up in a bun and skipped the makeup, put Thea's books in an old backpack, and headed downstairs.

I texted Thea: "How about dinner? What would you like?"

Thea texted back: "OK. Chinese."

I gave her a thumbs-up emoji and told her I'd be there as soon as I could.

———

I felt only a little better than I had at work—more like a wadded-up ball of paper than had been fished from the trash and tentatively decompressed, if not smoothed out—but at least getting Thea's agreement on dinner had started to turn things around. Like we were taking a first step together in a new direction.

Back when Thea's mom was dying, I longed to find words to comfort Thea, anything to make her laugh or believe it was going to be all right. I never found them, though; my brain filled with static any time my thoughts turned to her family. So most of our time together had been spent in silence. I'd never felt more inadequate in my whole life.

"I don't know what to do," I complained to my mother. "I never know what to say. I'm useless."

Mom continued peeling potatoes into the sink. "You're more help than you know," she said. "You're doing great, just being with Thea."

That was Mom being Mom. What else was she going to say?

When Mrs. Willis died, life continued being depressing for months, a different flavor of awful every week. Thea and her dad insisted I eat with them every Tuesday and Thursday night. It felt wrong, my helping to eat all the frozen casseroles Mom had organized, but you can't say no to someone whose wife or mother had just died. We sat in silence and chewed until someone sobbed. The first time, I tried to leave right away but both Thea and her dad grabbed my arms and held on tight. So I sat there watching them cry. We repeated that routine for weeks, offering up slight variations like the time we went out to dinner after taking Thea's mother's clothes to a women's shelter.

Thea sat in the booth, me next to her, both of us facing her dad and her little brother, Anthony. Tears and snot poured down everyone's faces.

"What can I get you?" the waitress asked Mr. Willis.

He opened his mouth and looked at us, but no sound came out. The waitress, recognizing a catastrophe unfolding, left us alone to consider our menu options. But the second time she came back, things weren't any better.

Mr. Willis stared at the menu with glassy eyes. Anthony spun the salt shaker around and around with his fingertip. Thea hugged her knees to her chest and stared at the ceiling.

"Everyone would like a plain hamburger," I said, choosing what seemed like the path of least resistance.

"You got it, baby doll," the waitress said.

The whole dinner was a moist affair, down to the glasses sweating onto the Formica tabletop. I sat next to the metal napkin dispenser, yanking out its contents nonstop. As we stood to go, I grabbed the last handful in the dispenser. We'd need them for the drive home, I suspected.

Crying makes you hungry, it turns out, so on the way home Mr. Willis stopped at the supermarket and bought two gallons of ice cream. At their house we sat around the table and devoured it right out of the carton—one for Mr. Willis and Anthony, one for Thea and me.

"Thanks for ordering the burgers for us, Jane," Mr. Willis said.

I shrugged. "You're welcome. It's not much."

"I hated walking through the restaurant. All those people watching me cry," Thea said.

"Forget about those people," Mr. Willis said. "They don't know you."

"They looked at me like I was being punished."

"We're all being punished," Anthony said. "Mom's dead."

"Shut up, Anthony!"

"Hush, now," Mr. Willis said. "Both of you."

Thea wrapped her arm through mine and squeezed. I squeezed back. When you're thirteen, there's not much else you can do.

———

Thea lived near the National Zoo. Her neighborhood had beautiful tall hardwood trees and Starbucks everywhere.

I crossed over Connecticut and waited for the bus headed back downtown. At the stop, I called the Chinese restaurant.

"Hi, I want to place a take-out order."

The guy on the other line shouted "Uh-huh." I could hear the background noise through the phone, even from a busy city street. Did they put the phone in the dead center of the kitchen?

"I want an order of vegetable fried rice,"—Thea's a

vegetarian now and always gets vegetable fried rice—"and an orange beef, two spring rolls, and two egg rolls."

"You want fried rice, not steamed?" I stuck my finger in my ear to drown out the street traffic.

"No, I want the steamed rice that comes with the beef, but I also want a vegetable fried rice."

"Vegetable fried rice, and an egg roll."

"Two egg rolls and two spring rolls. And an orange beef."

"Orange beef, okay. You want soup?"

"No, I do not want soup." I rolled my eyes at the other lady waiting at the bus stop, but she didn't pay me any attention.

"Name?"

"Desmond."

"What?"

"Desmond. D-E-S-M-O-N-D." I should have given Thea's name. I can't believe I just screamed my name on the city street.

"Five minutes," he said and hung up.

I got off the bus a few stops from Thea's and walked downhill to the restaurant.

"Take-out order for Desmond," I said.

The man at the counter looked through a pile of order tickets. "No Desmond."

"I called it in fifteen minutes ago," I said. "You said it would be ready in five minutes."

"It's not here," he said. "No order for Desmond."

"Okay." I took a deep breath. The smells coming from the kitchen made me super hungry, but I didn't want my hunger to fuel my temper. "Then let me place an order now."

"Yes," he said, pen at the ready.

"For Desmond. D-E-S-M-O-N-D. I want a vegetable—"

"Fried rice, right?" said a guy coming around the corner with a huge plastic bag. "Orange beef, veggie fried rice, egg rolls, spring rolls, hot and sour soup?" he asked. "You must be starving."

He was taller than me, and his hair was kind of longish and fell in his eyes. He flipped it out of his face with a twitch of his head and grinned. His teeth were perfect.

It took me a minute to remember I should answer him. "Um, it's not all for me." Which was the stupidest thing I could say; of course he knew it wasn't all for me. I always respond as if everyone is dead earnest. It's one of my least-endearing qualities.

But before I could say anything else he handed me my order. "Enjoy it," he said, and went back to the kitchen.

The man at the desk who took my order held out his hand for the ticket stapled to the bag. He rang it up, and I paid for it. Outside, I realized I bought soup I didn't want, but I couldn't go back and return soup. Especially not if that guy might see me trying to return soup; I'd look like a lunatic. So I took it to Thea's.

CHAPTER FOUR

———————

"Help has arrived!" I announced as Thea opened the door.

She stepped back to let me in. Unlike me, she kept her home so clean you could do surgery in her front hall. I put the bags of dinner on the table and spread the boxes out buffet-style. "I got your favorite, of course."

Thea shut the door and padded over to survey my selections. I glanced around the room. "Wow, look at all you've done," I said.

Even though she'd started packing, everything was tidy. Boxes sat stacked in a corner of the living room, numbered and labeled as to their contents and the room where they belonged in her new house. In the same situation, I'd save everything until the last minute, scoop whatever was nearby into a box, and spend the next six months opening cartons looking for that book I thought I'd bought or that receipt I needed.

"It's really happening," I said. "Just a few more weeks until you say good-bye to apartment living."

She nodded, poking her finger into a plastic bag. "I meant to ask you the other day, are you free tomorrow? Will you help me move some stuff?"

"Of course. I can't wait to see your new place. Now, how about some veggie fried rice?" I found two plates in the kitchen and opened the first white carton.

Thea walked over to the sofa and flopped down. "It was kind of you to bring me dinner, but I'm not hungry just now," she said, pulling a pillow into her lap.

Then why did she tell me to order it? Never mind, I thought. I picked up the cartons and put them in the fridge, then dropped my backpack next to the sofa and sat down beside her. She leaned her head back and closed her eyes.

"Don't fret." I massaged her hand between both of mine. "I know it's scary right now, but you're fantastic. You'll find a job in no time. And I'll help you. I'll do everything I can."

Thea smiled without opening her eyes. "I know you will, Jane."

"In fact," I said, reaching down for my backpack, "I got you something to kick off the search." I pulled the books out of my bag.

Thea lifted her head and cracked one eye at the noise I made, then sat up to shuffle through the books. I'd hidden the bounty hunter one on the bottom so she'd see it last. When she saw it, she burst out laughing.

"Is this a thing?"

"Bounty hunting? Yeah, of course," I said.

"No, I know that there are bounty hunters. I mean, do people actually buy books about how to become a bounty hunter? Do people *write* books on becoming a bounty hunter?"

"Apparently they do both."

"I guess the evidence is here in my hands." She flipped the pages, then looked up at me. "I owe you one, Jane. You've opened my eyes to a career possibility I never considered."

"I think you'd be awesome. I'd love to see you kicking in doors and dragging deadbeats out by their hair."

She smiled a half smile. "I might have to hit the gym a bit before I apply for that job."

"Well, that's a good thing, too. Manage your stress, right?"

"Yeah." She pulled her hand from mine and twisted the corner of the pillow back and forth.

It wasn't going to be easy to keep her spirits up. I knew that. But seeing her so defeated—well, to be honest, it frightened me. She had the right to feel depressed, of course, but something felt off. I couldn't put my finger on it.

You see, she's always been a fixer, a solver of problems. She's got a natural confidence that everything, absolutely everything, is within her grasp; it's as if she believes that she's been given the pieces of a puzzle to solve, so she applies herself and solves it. When confronted with a challenge, she's never backed down, not that I can remember. In fact, I've made a habit of studying her, knowing that if ever I found myself in a daunting situation, I'd have a clear roadmap to find my way; she'd have written it for me. So in a way, even though we're the same age, I've always considered Thea my mentor.

To give you an example, back when we were in high school, maybe in tenth grade, we were required to do a science fair project that counted for half our semester grade. I had conceived of a project on food preservatives and mold, and I devised tests to run on slices of bread and a block of cheddar cheese. I wasn't a great scientist, but I was mildly proud of it.

Everything was going great. I had weeks' worth of data and photos from the beginning and middle of the project. On a Saturday morning four days before the project was due, I came into the corner of our basement where I'd been running my experiment. I planned to take the final pictures and collect my last data points.

All my samples were gone.

Our beagle, Bosco, sat under the table, looking very much like he knew he'd done something wrong.

"Bosco!" I screamed. "Oh my God! My project! You ate my project! Bad dog! You are a very bad, BAD DOG!"

Bosco hung his head and looked up at me with his soft brown eyes.

"No!" I said. "I do NOT forgive you! It's not okay!"

My mom came downstairs. "What on earth is your problem?" she asked, wiping her hands on her apron. "What is—oh." She paused on the last step, looking at the empty table and the full dog.

"Bosco ate my project! It's half my grade! I'm going to

fail science because I don't have my final data. Who let him down here?"

"Oh, honey. It was probably me," she said, tucking her hair behind her ear. "I'm sorry. I came down here last night to get some ice cream out of the freezer, and I guess I didn't shut the door all the way."

"Mom! How could you?" Bosco was notorious for eating anything. He loved to eat underpants out of the laundry. He ate crayons and then pooped in vivid rainbow hues. We had to lock up the cat's litter box because he thought it was an all-you-can-eat buffet.

"I'm sorry, honey." She tried to give me a hug.

"I don't want a hug." I pushed her away. "You've ruined my science grade. I'm not going to get in to college because of this."

"Sweetheart, you're exaggerating."

"You don't understand!" I ran up the stairs. "I'm going to Thea's."

I fled down the block to Thea's house. She came to the door, still in her pajamas. I guess it was nine in the morning.

"Thea," I sobbed. "Bosco ate my science project."

She opened her arms and hugged me, patting my back while I slobbered on her shoulder.

"Sorry," I said when I came up for air. "Your shirt's pretty gross now."

She shrugged. "It's going in the wash anyway."

We went to the kitchen, where Thea's dad was making pancakes. "Hey, girls. Who's hungry?"

"Me," we said in unison.

He set two plates in front of us, stacked high and steaming. We drowned them in syrup and dug in.

"So," Thea said, cutting a perfectly sized bite with the edge of her fork. "Maybe there's a way to salvage this."

"How?" I asked. "All my data's gone."

"Not all your data," she pointed out. "Maybe we can research dogs' digestive systems and the species of mold you grew, and we can monitor Bosco for the next few days and see what happens."

"But what if nothing happens? Bosco has guts of steel."

Thea shrugged. "Sometimes experiments fail or don't produce the expected outcome. That's science. That's totally legitimate. I think we've got to take what we've got and creatively spin it to a new hypothesis and result. Don't give up," she said, tapping her forehead with a slender finger. "You know. Fight back, fight smarter." She grinned.

And just then, I felt my whole body relax. It would be a lot of work, for sure, but she'd saved me from failing science.

Thea changed out of the pajamas I'd slobbered on, and we went back to my house.

We took photos of the guilty party and weighed him on the bathroom scale. Then we took him to the vet for an emergency check and interviewed the doctor. I showed the photos from the middle of the project to the vet, which helped her to assess the risk of Bosco getting ill. Since my food had been growing bluish-green molds, we determined it was a species of *Penicillium*, which is where penicillin comes from. And since penicillin is prescribed to dogs as an antibiotic, and Bosco had only ingested a moderate amount of mold, we theorized that Bosco would suffer no ill effects.

As I wrote my final report, I noted that I only had a short time to observe the effects of Bosco's culinary exploits and that while a longer observational period would be ideal, ethical conflicts presented by animal research, especially on household pets, outweighed the needs of this project. I also noted the importance of securing the experiment site in future research.

Bosco had barfed in the car on the way to the vet but was fine after that. And I got an A on my project.

Thea's always been like that for me, my port in a storm. Though she's never brought it up, and she'd stop me if I did, I've always felt like she got the short end of the friendship stick. She'd argue I was there with her when her mom died, but honestly, sitting next to her like a stupid lump hardly seems like a valuable service rendered. She, on the other hand, has solved genuine problems for me. I admire that about her, her skill in fixing things.

I'd longed for the opportunity to pay her back for all the times she'd nursed me through my personal dramas. Now, seeing her curled on her sofa depressed and uncertain, I felt a weird kind of relief. Finally, here was my chance.

"Thea," I said. "I can't bear to see you so anxious."

She shrugged and curled her knees in tighter to her thin body.

The two of us sat in silence. I watched as, with a long, beautifully manicured fingernail, she worked a hole in the hem of her jeans and wormed her finger inside, rending the hole larger and larger.

"Stop," I said. "You're ruining your jeans."

She persisted.

"Come on." I tugged her hand away. "Let's eat some dinner. That'll make you feel better." I ran to fix her a plate of rice with two spring rolls, grabbed a fork and napkin from the kitchen, and brought it to her, though she doesn't like to eat on her sofa.

"Just put it there," she said, gesturing to the floor in front of the sofa with her toe.

I did as I was told. She refused to look at me.

As we faced off—or not; she stared at a spot in the middle of the room—my stomach growled. The sound filled the living room. The corner of Thea's mouth ticked up.

"You can eat," she said, stretching and recoiling on the sofa. "Just because I'm being dull doesn't mean you can't enjoy your dinner."

I shifted my weight from one foot to the other. "Will you come to the table and sit with me, at least?"

"Bring your food in here." She curled into the fetal position.

I filled a plate with orange beef and rice and sat down on the floor, crossing my legs like a kindergartener. The ticking of an old desk clock of her father's filled the room, a metronome measuring the meter of traffic, the noise from neighboring apartments, scoring each moment of Thea's paralysis.

If my heart set the tone instead, we'd be flying through the evening. "What are you most worried about?" I asked.

"The house, I guess. Between earnest money and deposits on services, I'm feeling cash poor. I mean, I have some severance, but I've got to get things moved, cleaned out here…" She shook her head. "I don't want to think about it tonight."

She released a slender arm from where she'd hugged her knees and brought it up as if to make a pillow for her head. She couldn't fool me: Thea meant to hide and wipe away the tears forming in the corners of her eyes. Though her body had always been petite, she'd never looked fragile. She'd always been tough as a prize fighter. Tonight, she looked down for the count.

I thought about the science fair disaster, and how she'd taken control and shown me a way out. The science fair wasn't on the same scale as losing a job, but then again, she'd picked me up countless times over the years, for all sorts of pathetic woes. Nothing I'd done for her approached all the help she'd given me. I owed her. And now was my chance.

"I'm not going to let you lose your house," I said. "No way. We'll do this one step at a time. Sit up and eat some dinner."

Thea slid obediently to the floor and picked up her plate. She leaned back against the sofa and put a forkful of rice in her mouth.

She managed half a smile. "Okay," she said, nodding. "Yeah, that's good. You can always count on the Jade Palace to deliver."

"Ha. You can always count on *Jane* to deliver."

She rolled her eyes, but the corners of her mouth twitched.

Now we were getting somewhere. "Listen," I said. "Let me help you with the job search. The conventional wisdom says it's all about networking. I can help you with that. You've got tons of connections in the industry. Tell me who to call and I'll call them for you. Just until you're feeling yourself again."

She shook her head and moved the vegetables around on her plate. "I'd rather not think about it now."

"But you—"

"Maybe later. Look, I know you want to help, and you can help me with the networking, but let's give it a day or two." She stabbed a bamboo shoot, the tines of her fork clicking against the porcelain plate.

I had to tread carefully. But I caught a glimpse of the real Thea in there, the fighter I knew. I picked up an egg roll.

"How's your mom?" Thea asked.

"Oh, you know. Still trying to fix me up with anyone single, male, and breathing."

She snorted.

"Speaking of Jade Palace delivering," I said, swallowing another bite of egg roll, "they've got a really cute guy working there now. I hope he's doing deliveries. I'll be ordering a lot more frequently if that's the case."

"Oh, really?" Thea raised an eyebrow at me. "Details, please."

"He's taller than me."

"Good start." Thea scooped up another forkful of rice.

"And he's got longish brown hair. Not so long that it's sloppy or a health issue."

"Was he wearing a sexy hairnet?"

"Ew. No. He wasn't cooking. He's got big brown eyes and a nice smile. When he brought the food he made a joke about how I must be really hungry, and I said, 'No, no, it's not all for me,' and—"

Thea started to laugh. "You always do that."

"I know! I didn't realize until after the fact that he was teasing, that he knew it wasn't all for me. So unfortunately, now he thinks I'm a moron." My stomach felt twisty. I was glad to have Thea smiling again, but thinking about Delivery Guy made me despair for myself. Would I ever outgrow this social incompetence?

"He doesn't think you're a moron."

"Let's hope not. I'll have to prepare myself for the next time I see him."

"You don't have to prepare anything. Just be yourself. You're charming."

"Aw, thanks." And there she was, picking me up again.

"Oh. Remember how last week you wanted me to ask Richard if he had any single friends he could set you up with?" she said. "I did ask. He said he'd think about it. But you might want to set up an online dating profile. It's not horrible, I promise. It's how I met Richard."

Okay, so it's true I think Thea could do better than Richard. But I wasn't above asking him to set me up. Anything would be better than online dating.

"I'd rather meet someone through friends."

"Or accidentally? Like this delivery guy? Maybe you don't need a setup after all." She smirked.

When she said it out loud, it sounded ridiculous. I'm thirty-five; I can't get melty about some guy who delivers food for a living. It might have been okay in high school or early college. But now—I needed to find someone with a career. An equal partner.

I tried to brush it off. "Forget that. He thinks I'm an idiot. I'm here to help you, not to whine about my social ineptitude."

"I like talking about your social ineptitude," Thea said, flashing her grin. "It's one of my favorite topics."

"I like making plans of action," I said. "Having a plan is the best way to avoid anxiety. Let's brainstorm." I jumped up and ran to Thea's desk, where I grabbed a Sharpie and a legal pad from the top drawer. "Let's figure out some steps to take that will make you feel more at ease until you're back on your feet for good." I grabbed one of the job books and found the table of contents.

Thea deflated like a pricked balloon. "Jane, I appreciate what you're trying to do for me. Really, I do. But tonight, what I'd like most is to not think about work at all." She took her empty plate to the kitchen, rinsed it, and put it in her dishwasher. "Are you done, or do you want more?" she asked, nodding at the food on the table.

"I don't know."

"Why don't…why don't we sit on the couch and eat ice cream out of the carton and watch a sappy movie?"

Just like that, she'd fallen back into her pit again. Thea collapsed onto the sofa and reached for the remote control on the side table. What was going on with her? Sitting and doing nothing was only for times of utter security. She was a planner, a thinker, not a procrastinator. Not a couch potato. That was my job.

Not anymore. Now my job was to guide her through. What would Thea do if the roles were reversed? She'd tell me to fight; that had been her mantra for years. "Fight harder. Fight smarter." She'd never let me wallow in anything, not for a second.

"I know it's scary, Thea," I said, hoping my voice sounded both soothing and firm, and hid the panic I felt rising in my rib cage. "But I've known you all my life. You'll feel better once you have a plan. We don't have to nail everything down tonight. Let's think about how to get through the next two weeks. That's manageable, right? How much money do you have in the bank?"

"That's none of your business!" Thea snapped, throwing the remote control to the floor. "Look. If you want to be a friend, sit down and watch a movie with me, okay? My life's not going to fall apart in the next twenty-four hours. I just don't want to think about it right now. Am I not entitled to feel a little bit sad and anxious about this?"

"Sure you are. But, Thea, this isn't like you at all."

"Well, I've never been fired from a job before."

"It's not your fault."

"I know it's not my fault. But it still sucks."

"I'm not arguing that. This came out of nowhere, and it's completely unjust. But don't you…don't you want to fight back?" My legs felt jumpy. I got up to pace the room. "Wouldn't you sleep better at night, having a plan in place about the house?"

"I thought you wanted to help me." Thea's voice quivered. She glared at me, arms folded across her chest.

"I do! I am helping you."

"No, frankly you're making it worse."

"What?" She completely misunderstood me. "How am I making it worse?"

"You're trying to make me think about things I'm not prepared to think about right now."

I rolled my eyes. "For God's sake, Thea. Of course I am. But that's not making it worse, that's making it better. You've never been one to take things lying down. Like you've always said, 'Fight harder, fight smarter.' You've said that for ages."

"You don't get to say that to me."

The ice in her voice brought goose bumps to my arms. Her dark eyes flashed at me, and though her jaw was set, her lips quivered.

"Thea," I murmured, opening my arms to hug her. We'd get through this together.

"You know," Thea said, crossing the room to the apartment door, "maybe it's better if you leave." She put her hand on the doorknob. "Thank you for bringing dinner. You're right. It did help."

My jaw dropped to my stomach. My stomach plunged to my knees. "You're throwing me out?"

"Actually, I've made a plan. For tonight. I'm going to watch a little TV and go to bed early," she said, opening the door for me. "You're right. I do feel better."

No part of my body would perform its job. My ears buzzed; Thea sounded far away. My muscles couldn't move my legs or my arms. My mouth couldn't form words. I just took up space in her room.

Thea tipped her head toward the door, gently, like a ballet dancer's gesture.

I obeyed, lifting my backpack to my shoulder and reaching for my dinner plate.

"You don't have to do that," she said, her voice back to its normal tone. "I'll clean up. And take the books, too."

"You don't want them?"

"They'll get lost in the move. Keep them safe for me."

I grabbed my shoes and stumbled to the door. "I didn't mean any harm, Thea."

"I'll talk to you later," she said and closed the door.

CHAPTER FIVE

I stood there in the dim light of the hall, on the worn blue carpet, with my shoes in one hand and my backpack dangling off one shoulder.

She threw me out.

I don't remember putting my shoes back on, but I was wearing them when I left her building. I walked down the leaf-shrouded sidewalk toward Connecticut Avenue, trying to figure out what just happened.

It had to be a shock, of course, losing your job so suddenly. That accounted, at least in part, for her strange behavior. I pictured Rita, my boss's boss and the publisher of *Recycling World*, marching into the office and telling everyone to clean out their desks. The folds of powdery flesh hanging off her jaw quivered with delight as she contemplated her upcoming promotion, while the rest of us queued up at job fairs, piles of resumes growing damp and smudged in our sweaty hands. As I stood on the twilit sidewalk waiting for the bus to take me home, I pictured myself walking out of my office building with a large cardboard box as passing strangers smirked at me. People who didn't even know me made assumptions about my worth, my conduct, my intellect, my basic competence, as they hustled along to their next client meeting, their next appointment or conference.

I felt my face grow hot. Tears stung my eyes. The bus pulled up and I climbed aboard, my body on autopilot. In my mind I came home to my little apartment, half-packed boxes piled everywhere as I prepared to move to my first real home, a home I'd saved for, now owned, and could do with as I liked. I pictured myself on the floor, leaning against the moving boxes, staring at my closing statement in one hand (a six-figure balance) and my bank statement in the other (a three-figure balance).

The jerk of the bus pulling away from the curb yanked me back into the moment. I tried to swallow, but my tongue filled my mouth. The muscles at the base of my throat tightened, and my hand rose to my collarbone, massaging it gently. I concentrated on taking deep breaths. I was only imagining things. It wasn't real. Not for me.

"Are you okay, dear?" An elderly lady in a pale blue cardigan leaned forward and patted my shoulder.

"Yes, I'm fine. Thank you," I said. "I was just thinking about my dear friend. She lost her job." I wiped my face with the back of my hand and smiled at her.

"Oh, that's terrible," she agreed, sitting back in her seat. She stared out the window at the lights of the restaurants and laundromats we passed by.

Poor Thea! I hadn't even lost my job and here I was, crying on the bus from daydreaming about it. I sagged in my seat, feeling drained. No wonder she felt so over-whelmed.

Snippets of our conversation played again and again in my mind.

Why don't we sit on the couch and eat ice cream out of the carton and watch a sappy movie?

Like you've always said, 'Fight harder, fight smarter.' You've said that for ages.

You don't get to say that to me.

Why wouldn't I get to say that to her? She's told me that dozens of times. It's such a part of her identity, it's practically tattooed on her arm.

Across the aisle, a toddler started to fuss.

"Come here, baby girl. You're tired," her mother said, pulling the girl into her lap. The child lay her head against her mother's shoulder and stuck her thumb into her mouth.

I watched the toddler, in striped leggings and a T-shirt adorned with ladybugs, sag beneath the bright lights over-head. The largest ladybug, appliquéd in satin, rested on her stomach. The girl rubbed the satin with her unsucked thumb as she worked the other one, her eyelids falling, blocking out the fluorescent glare.

Come here, baby girl.

Mrs. Willis raised a battered arm from the cotton hospital blanket and beckoned to Thea. Thea got up from the padded visitor's chair in the corner and sat on the thinly cushioned metal stacking chair next to the bed, taking her mother's hand in hers. Mrs. Willis's fingers looked like a bouquet of twigs in Thea's smooth, healthy young fist.

"Baby girl, promise me one thing," Mrs. Willis said.

"Yes, Mama?"

"Promise me you will always be a fighter. The world is hard and ugly sometimes. You have to fight to stay happy, fight to stay healthy. Fight for what is true and good. Fight for those you love, but most importantly, I want you to fight for yourself and your dreams. You understand me?"

If Thea said anything, I couldn't hear. I stood outside the door, juggling two large cups of chipped ice and grape juice in my hands, fresh from the nurses' station. It was wrong to eavesdrop, true, but even back then I understood that neither was it the time to bust in and dispense refreshments.

"I fought this cancer so I could have a chance to be with you and Anthony and your dad as long as I could. I may not make it, but I promise I will fight for every day I can get with you. Life is going to throw nasty things at you from time to time. You have to fight back at it. When you get knocked down, fight harder. Fight smarter. Use that beautiful, brilliant mind of yours."

Thea murmured something. I heard her start to cry.

"Climb up here with me, baby girl," Mrs. Willis said. Through the door, the hospital bed squeaked and rustled. "The world can be hard, and I want you to fight, but— listen to me, listen to me. The world can be awfully good, too. It's filled with good people, kind people. Love them and let them love you back. People want to take care of you. Let them. Then you take care of them in your turn."

She had paused then. I remember standing in the hall,

thinking I should knock, but then I heard them continuing their conversation, in softer voices. I shuffled back and forth, watching their ice melt.

———

What had she said in that quieter conversation? It would come to me later, probably. I remember thinking how Mrs. Willis, who was usually so independent, had let my family take care of her and hers. How I'd wanted to help Thea, and I hadn't known how.

Well, that was long ago. I had more resources now, more ideas, more ways to be of support. Maybe tonight had been too soon. She was shocked and exhausted; a weekend of rest would surely get her back on track. I'd leave her alone for a few days.

I pictured my mom on the phone with everyone who knew the Willises, the receiver tucked between her ear and shoulder, making notes on a calendar with a ballpoint pen. The Thompsons would bring baked ham on Tuesday, the Cohns would bring lasagna on Thursday, we'd have them over on Saturday. Everyone on the PTA roster, their tennis league; Mom dragging Dad's Rotary Club directory out of the drawer and making another list. "Jane, we'd be lost without your mother," Mr. Willis said. And as the bus pulled along up the hill, nearing my stop, a plan formed in my head.

———

Back in my apartment, I kicked off my shoes and turned

on my computer. Dishes from breakfast sat in the sink, but I had more important work to do.

Without knowing Thea's financial circumstances, I couldn't help her budget, but there were other ways I could take care of her. Developing a preliminary job-search strategy seemed the most useful approach. Kind of like the way she'd mapped out an alternative route with the science fair, I could map out simple tasks to help her get back on the road to employment. I had the energy for it now, and she did not, but when she felt ready, she could approve my plans and take off like a rocket.

I logged in to the DC public library and checked out several more books on job hunting strategies. I downloaded them to my phone, put on an old T-shirt and brushed my teeth, put the books I'd purchased for Thea on my nightstand, then crawled into bed and began to read. I know, I'm not supposed to be on my phone before bedtime—studies say it makes it harder to fall asleep—but it was a minor sacrifice to make for my best friend.

I kept notes as I read:

1. **Update Thea's Resume.** I couldn't do it myself, of course, but I could do the typing for her, if she told me what to write.

2. **Tell Thea's Network.** All the books emphasized the importance of alerting everyone in your personal network of your job-search intentions. *Put your friends to work for you!* the books demanded. A bit awkward, I thought, but the books probably had a point. I admired how Thea had more than one thousand friends on Facebook—all of them real. Everyone she met wanted to connect closely to her. A quick status update from Thea, and she'd have one thou-

sand people looking out for her. Again, Thea could tell me what to say, and I could handle this for her. She'd had me post on her behalf before, like the time she was baking a cake and needed emergency advice, but her hands were sticky.

3. **Develop an Elevator Pitch**. Another thing these books had in common was that they were enamored of something called an "elevator pitch." According to the books, this seemed to be a thirty-second summary of your personal skills and career ambitions. The idea was that you could drop the speech on someone in an elevator before they clawed at the button panel to be let off.

This seemed like a terrible idea; I mean, who wants to be assaulted with a personal ad from a stranger in an elevator? But four different books stressed the importance of having an elevator pitch, so it went on the to-do list.

My brain hummed with ideas and plans, and a flurry of notepaper blanketed my nightstand and slid to the floor beside my bed. I looked at the clock, dismayed to see it was 3:45 a.m. If I didn't stop now, I'd be useless to Thea tomorrow. Or today, I guess. So I put the phone down and turned off my light. I felt good; I felt like I was actually solving a problem, for a change.

I tried to get comfortable, but whether I lay on my back or my side or my stomach, I couldn't relax. It was wildly unfair, what happened to Thea and her colleagues. It seemed that every week I read a news article about people losing their jobs to cheaper labor or to technology. I don't mean blue-collar jobs—the kinds of jobs that used to be plentiful in places like Bishop's Creek, where Thea and I grew up. Sam, my friend who lives in the bank doorway, is a case in point. He worked in a furniture plant years ago, applying varnishes to tables and desks, and when his factory shut down he made do for a time, but then he lost his house, then his car. He hitchhiked here and stayed with a friend from the army until the friend got drunk one night and tried to kill him. He's been at the bank doorway ever since.

But those types of layoffs have been happening for decades. It's the reason neither Thea nor I returned to Bishop's Creek after college: no prospects. What happened to Thea, well, I suppose I knew that it happened from time to time, but it never felt like something that would happen to anyone close to me.

Not long ago, I read an article in *Wired* predicting that within five years, computers would be able to read X-rays with incredible precision, doing some of the diagnostic work radiologists now did. I couldn't fathom it. What would I do if I'd spent years in medical school and accumulated hundreds of thousands of dollars of debt, only to be replaced by a machine a few years in? Who knew what other advances were just around the corner?

I watched shadows play across my ceiling; the light from the parking lot behind my building wedged through the leaves on the trees and the slats of my blinds. There's no more lonely time than four in the morning, and I knew I wasn't thinking logically but I couldn't turn my mind off. Jobs that once didn't require a college degree now demanded one. "Credential inflation," it was called. I had a graduate degree—not that I needed one—but I didn't feel any better protected.

My stomach churned. I should make a plan for myself

as long as I was helping Thea. Heaven knew, any idiot could manage *Recycling World.*

———

The next morning, I gathered up the notepaper avalanche from my bedside and dumped it on the kitchen table. Over my standard breakfast, a bowl of Frosted Flakes and a pot of strong black coffee, I assembled them into an action plan, complete with step-by-step bullet points and calendar dates by which to take the actions.

I drained the milk from my bowl and perused the *InStyle* that came the day before. The irony is not lost on me that I subscribe to a magazine called *InStyle*—in fact, I look forward to its arrival every month—yet most of my clothes are old enough to have a driver's license.

I should be beyond caring about fashion and clothes. What matters, I keep reminding myself, is what's on the inside. Unfortunately, that idea, like much of the contents of *InStyle*, is more aspirational than realistic. So I keep reading. Maybe I'll reconcile all these issues one day— probably when I'm eighty and can't remember where I live, much less what the must-have handbag of the season looks like.

Mom's ringtone, the *wah-wah-wah* trombone sound that stands in for adult speech in Peanuts cartoons, heralded this week's guilt-laden conversation. She gets antsy if she doesn't hear from me every few days. You'd think by now she'd have learned to let go a little, but it could be worse; I have friends from college whose parents call or text them several times a day. Can you imagine?

"Hi, Mom."

"Hello, sugar. I hadn't talked to you in a while, and I just wanted to see how you are."

"I'm fine," I said, topping off my bowl with a few more Frosted Flakes. "Just eating breakfast. Hope you don't mind."

"No, of course not. So. What's new?"

"Nothing with me. But Thea lost her job. They down-sized her whole department."

"Oh, how terrible! How's she doing?"

"She's in shock. But I'm trying to help. Gathering information for her so when she's ready she can leap into action."

"Well, that's very kind of you, dear. Just remember to give her some space."

"Yeah," I said, taking my coffee cup back to the pot for a refill. Then I stopped. "Wait. What's that supposed to mean?"

"Well," Mom said. I recognized that *well*; it was the prelude to an argument. "You have a tendency, dear. It comes from a good place, of wanting to be supportive. But sometimes you can...well, you know."

"No. I don't know. What do you mean?"

"Darling, you tend to lay it on a bit thick."

"A bit thick?"

"You mean to be helpful, but sometimes you can be... too much." She sighed. "I don't know how I let you get this way."

"So I'm bossy?"

"Not bossy, not really. Just...suffocating."

"Suffocating?!" I shoved my coffee cup back onto the

table a little more forcefully than I meant to. Coffee slopped over the side and stained the edge of last month's *Cosmopolitan*. She always did this. Every time she called she found something to criticize. I wanted to pace but my kitchen's too small to offer satisfactory relief. I ended up bouncing back and forth like a metronome arm. "What do you mean, suffocating? That's a terrible thing to say."

"It's my fault, dear. I should have done a better job teaching you."

"I'm not suffocating anyone," I screamed. "I totally respect people's privacy."

"I don't mean—"

"You do mean. But you don't know what you're talking about. Thea's my best friend. She's always supported me when I've been upset. She's done a thousand things for me over the years, and I've never been able to repay her. Now I have a chance to do something for her in exchange. I mean, she just closed on her house and then *wham!*, she lost her job. Do you have any idea how stressful that is?"

"I'm sure it's terrible, darling. I only meant—"

"She's going to pieces. She's absolutely paralyzed. I can't bear it. I went over to her apartment last night, and all she wanted to do was veg out on the sofa and watch movies."

"Well, honey, that's not such a bad thing."

"She's got mortgage payments coming! All the plans she made this past year were predicated on having a stable income. A few months ago their director was saying what a great job they'd done and how everything was looking terrific for the next quarter. She didn't see this coming at all. The least I can do is support her while she's falling apart."

"Of course you should support her. I'm not saying you shouldn't. But there's more than one way to do that."

"You aren't here. You can't see her. You don't know what she needs."

Mom sighed. "No. You're right about that."

I hated when she got like this, when she sighed at me. She wasn't admitting I was right; she was bored and wanted to get off the phone.

Me too, but I learned back in high school that hanging up on Mom tends to get repaid in a tax of extra guilt. I had to find a way to make nice with her and then devise an excuse to hang up. I picked up my dishes and added them to the sink's current residents. I'd clean everything up later. "What's new with you and Dad, then?"

Mom sighed again. "Well, not much. We've taken up tennis again—the doctor said we're not getting enough exercise, so we've joined a seniors group at the Y. We do a mixed-doubles round-robin tournament all summer. None of us care about actually winning the tournament, so we don't keep track. We just want to be more active."

I sat back down and rested my forehead on the table. This was going to take forever. "That sounds nice."

"It is. And Patty Alexander told me last week that her son, Paul—you remember him?—he's moving to the DC area sometime this month. I gave her your phone number to give to him."

There it was, as predictable as DC's summer humidity and just as welcome. If I'm still single in another thirty-five years, and if I don't strangle her first, she'll still be trying to set me up. I pictured her at the assisted-living home, age ninety-five, smiling up from her wheelchair at the new fellow who just moved in. "I've got a daughter about your age."

"Mom, I don't need you to set me up."

"I'm not setting you up. He may not even call you. It's just so he'll know someone in the area."

"It's a big area. I'm sure he's got friends from college who are here."

"Well, you're probably right, and like I said, he probably won't call. But it's nice to have a contact from home. You know. Just in case you need it."

I couldn't imagine why a grown man would need the comfort of someone he last saw in eighth grade, but I couldn't debate the issue further. As she did every week, she'd crushed my will to live.

"Okay. Well, have fun with your tennis tournament. I have to go. I'm helping Thea move to her new house."

"Of course. Remember to give her space. Love you, darling. Call me next week."

"I will, Mom." She'd call me first.

"Bye-bye."

"Bye."

If there was one good thing about my remaining single and childless, it must be that I was doing a service to humanity by not nagging my child the way Mom nagged me. Did other mothers tell their adult kids how to live? Was it an inevitable part of being a parent, a need to continue to form and reshape the life you'd created even when your project was, at least theoretically, finished?

I'd probably never know. Then again, no one could blame me for the next generation's dysfunction. My hands are clean. I swallowed the last of my coffee, threw on some old running shorts and a T-shirt, put my job-search outlines in my backpack, and went to catch the bus to Thea's apartment.

CHAPTER SIX

On the bus ride to Thea's, I made a mental plan. I wouldn't bring up the job hunt before lunch. Then I'd casually put out some feelers, see what she was thinking, and I would present my plan, bit by bit. I wouldn't drag out the bullet points unless she seemed receptive.

"Hi!" I said when she opened the door. "What do you want me to do first?"

Thea wore a grubby T-shirt and had pulled her hair back from her face. She also wore a baseball cap, which she only ever does if she's serious about getting filthy. She pointed to a mountain of boxes against the wall.

"We've got to move those to the house today, and then as much small furniture as we can manage. Chairs, side tables, lamps, things like that. And clothes—I've got suit-cases packed in the bedroom."

The U-Haul van was parked in the alley behind her building. By ten thirty we'd reduced the wall of boxes by half, so we drove the load out to her new townhouse. Thea unlocked the door and pushed it open.

"My home," she said with pride in her voice.

I adored it instantly. It was built in a quasi-Craftsman style, with a slate-tile entry and a long hallway leading to a bright, open family room and kitchen. As I walked down the hall, I imagined myself moving into such a place. I could decorate it with adult furniture and sell my dorm leftovers to poor college students who needed them. I could actually have a dog. Or maybe two.

"Those boxes are going upstairs," Thea said. "At the top of the stairs, there's a door ahead of you to the right. Put them in there." She went back outside.

On the left just before the family room, a compact staircase led up to the second floor. I climbed the steps and found two small bedrooms that would be perfect for an office and a guest room. The rooms shared a bathroom and each had a closet. I dropped the box in the middle of the floor, set my backpack down beside it, and opened the closet door.

Oh my God, it was a huge walk-in. This closet was bigger than my apartment's bathroom. I could actually stand in it and stretch my arms out to the side, and not touch the walls. It practically begged to be sublet.

"Thea, this closet is unbelievable!"

Thea appeared in the doorway, beaming. "It's amazing, right? I think I bought this place for the closets alone."

"It's breathtaking." Our voices bounced off the hardwood floors and echoed in the empty space. "Hello!" I called.

Thea rolled her eyes. "Come on. We have lots more to move."

Most of the book boxes came upstairs to her study, but a few went into the family room. The family room had a fireplace that actually burned wood. We could put Thea's big sofa in front of the fireplace, arrange a coffee table in front of it and a cozy armchair on either side. In a few months, she'd build a fire in the hearth, grab a couple of fuzzy blankets and big pillows, light some candles on the mantel. Fill a big glass of wine and snuggle down deep into the cushions with a book as the snow fell outside. What bliss!

Light from the tall dining-room windows bounced off the glossy hardwood floors and flashed in my eyes. Thea, as always, had made the right decision. Not only was the home suited to her personal style, it was an ideal match for her stage in life. The lingering aroma of fresh paint smelled to me like sweet success. What did I have to show for my thirteen years at *Recycling World*? A hand-me-down bed lofted on cinderblocks, apartment walls that hadn't been painted since I moved in, and, next to my aged futon, an impressive array of budget-conscious home storage systems containing unopened magazine subscription offers and college course notes I hadn't consulted since graduation.

"Ready to make a second run?" Thea asked, brushing her hands on the seat of her pants.

"Thea," I said, hoping she didn't pick up on the quiver in my voice, "this place is unbelievable. It's so perfect. Can you just imagine? Tucking into your sofa in front of a fire, with a fuzzy blanket and a book? I'd never leave."

"It's going to be wonderful." She gave herself a little hug.

"It is."

"Come on," she said. "Let's go get some furniture this time."

We locked up the house behind us and got back into the moving van. The upholstery felt itchy on the back of my legs.

Thea turned on the radio as we drove back into DC, but I didn't notice what was playing. All I could think about was Thea's amazing new home and how perfect it was for her, and how happy I was for her to move in. Thea loved to entertain. In a few weeks, she'd throw dinner parties or casual cookouts in the backyard. She'd always been gracious and loved to make people feel welcome and at ease. I imagined her circulating around the house, introducing guests to one another and pouring glasses of wine for newcomers. Her eyes sparkled and her smile was wide and warm. She glowed.

She couldn't lose the house.

The clock on the dashboard read 11:50. I'd promised myself I wouldn't bring up the job issue until after lunch. I'd promised. Thea sang along to the radio; the breeze from the window rushed over her face. I didn't want to risk it. But my stomach gnawed at me.

Back at the apartment, Thea looked around. "I'd rather do furniture this time. The boxes wore me out. Okay if we mix it up? Let's make a run with furniture, and then we can get lunch. I bet I'll have more energy for these boxes after I eat."

"Exactly what I was thinking," I said, which wasn't true, but I wished it were.

We gathered chairs, lamps, and small side tables and took them downstairs. We got so excited we decided to move a few larger items, including a desk and her dining table. We got downstairs with the desk and realized we stank at packing furniture.

"The desk should go in first," Thea said. "We need to put it toward the cab because of the weight." So we took everything out of the van and put it in the alley, then loaded the desk in first. We stacked stuff on top of the desk, wedged the dining table in, and shoved more things under the table.

My shirt was absolutely soaked through. "Ugh. I'm so gross."

Thea wiped her face with the hem of her T-shirt. It must have been ninety-five degrees in the shade of the alley.

We looked at each other. "Let's get a suitcase each," she said, "and we'll grab some water and go. We'll take it slowly at the house. I just want to make the most of the van while I have it."

"I'm with you."

"You sure you don't mind? Do you have anything else to do today?"

"No, not really." The only other thing I'd do was continue to plan her job search, but frankly, I preferred to play in her new house.

"Jane, you're the best," she said, giving me a moist hug. "Sorry I'm disgusting."

I returned the hug. Her hair smelled like rosemary and mint and sweat.

This time at the house, we decorated. Thea considered the placement of tables and lamps. "I need some rugs," she said. "We'll have to go shopping sometime."

"No hurry, though," I said. Rugs were expensive.

We placed an arm chair adjacent to the fireplace, and set the coffee table in front of it. Thea's nightstand went in her bedroom, her dining table in the breakfast nook of the kitchen. We hauled the desk upstairs to the study and pushed it against the wall opposite the stacks of books.

"Thea," I said, "it's starting to look like a home."

She flashed her beautiful grin, and for just a second she jumped up and down like a child. "My home! My real home!"

I glanced out the window onto the backyard. "Oh my gosh. You have a patio and a garage?"

"Yes. I've got to get a grill. I can't wait to have you and Narin over for a cookout."

"And you need a lawnmower." The grass looked desperate in the noonday heat. "And a hose and a sprinkler."

"The joys of home ownership. And I'm going to have to paint, too."

More money. But she didn't seem stressed.

"What's in the backpack?" she asked. "You've hauled that around with you all day."

"Oh. Well, it's just some ideas I put together for you." I slipped over to the backpack and pulled out a sheaf of legal paper. "I wasn't going to bring it up yet, but since you asked...It's a job-search task list. Last night I read those books and outlined a plan for you. Of course you can mix it up if you want," I said, hoping to relieve the aston-ishment on her face. "It's easy. See? It's a series of small tasks, so nothing's overwhelming."

"Is that all that's in there?" she asked, glancing over my shoulder.

"I left the books at my house, like you asked. I didn't want to overwhelm you. Why don't I leave it here, and you can go through it at your own pace? Of course I'm here to talk, anytime. I'll support you any way you like. I'll even help with the networking, like you said. That's the worst part, isn't it?" I wrinkled my nose, hoping to make light of it.

Thea shifted her weight from one foot to the other, turning the stapled pages.

"Come on, it's roasting." She pushed the yellow paper to the back of her desk. "Let's go get something to eat."

In the suitcases, Thea had packed some clean shirts and towels. We each went into a bathroom (she had two bath-rooms!) to clean up and put on a fresh T-shirt. I gagged a little when I put my sweaty bra and underwear back on, but the fresh T-shirt made me feel a bit better.

"There's a good place a few blocks from here," she said. "If you don't mind walking. It's got lots of healthy stuff."

Thea took me to a restaurant in a newish shopping devel-opment designed to look old. Tin tiles in a floral relief pattern covered the restaurant's ceilings, and from a large center medallion hung a whitewashed iron chandelier. The chairs were upholstered in colorful, quirky prints of old-fashioned canned goods and kitchen gadgets. The place looked like a girly version of an old-time grocery store, with cases full of prepared salads and distressingly caloric desserts. I loved it instantly.

"What's good?" I asked Thea as we side-shuffled our way past the cases. "The fruit salad looks exactly like what I want. And the bow-tie pasta. And the corn-and-bean-and-pepper thing."

"You'd like the chicken salad. And the roasted salmon."

"Oh my God, I'm never going to leave."

"And you haven't even gotten to the lemon bars," Thea said.

We set ourselves up at a table by the window, and I took a long gulp of strawberry lemonade. It was real, not from a powdered mix. I felt my dehydrated cells expand like a pop-up sponge submerged in a bath.

"I didn't realize moving was so much fun," Thea said. "I've been dreading it, actually."

"Why?"

"I keep uncovering new tasks I need to do or items to buy. You know, like you were saying. The hose and sprinkler and whatnot. Every time I step in the door I notice something else. But it will all happen in time."

"Sure."

"And it can wait until I get back from vacation." She sat back against the brightly patterned upholstery and smiled. "A week from today, I'll be dipping my toes in the beautiful Carribbean."

My mouth dropped open. "You'll be doing what?"

Thea wiggled her eyebrows at me. "I booked myself two weeks in the Virgin Islands. Just the sun, the sand, and some solitude."

What was she thinking? "Are you crazy?"

"Excuse me?"

I felt like an invisible hand gripped my throat. I tried to swallow, but despite the strawberry lemonade my mouth was parched. "Sorry. I mean, I'm astonished. You just lost your job and bought a house. Is now really the time to spend two weeks on an island?"

"I thought you'd be happy for me."

"I'm happy that you have your house. I'm happy to help you move in and to help you paint or whatever you need. But really, shouldn't you be hunting for a new job?"

She turned away from me. "I think I can manage myself."

My heart raced. She was out of control. She needed an intervention as much as she needed a job.

"Can you even afford this? Do you have the money?"

Thea sat up very straight and looked down her nose at me. "We've had this conversation before, Jane. My finances are none of your business."

"I'm not asking for amounts. I'm asking you to think about this. For heaven's sake! Vacations are expensive. You have mortgage payments to make. Rugs to buy! You literally just said you have dozens of things you've got to take care of, and they all cost money. How can you go tripping off to the islands? And for two whole weeks?"

"Maybe there's a part of me you don't know about."

"Like what, you're a secret millionaire? I'm shocked,

Thea. Stunned. This is the most irresponsible thing I think I've ever seen you do."

The waiter walked up with a huge tray. "Vegetarian bow-tie pasta?"

Thea raised her hand and smiled at the waiter. "Thank you."

"And this must be yours," he said, setting before me a stunning chicken salad croissant and a pile of fresh fruit. In the case, it looked mouth-watering, but I didn't feel hungry anymore.

"Anything else I can get you, ladies?" he asked, bending forward to hear us clearly.

"No, thank you," I said.

"Fresh ground pepper?"

Thea shook her head.

"Refills on drinks?"

"We'll wave you down if we need anything. Thank you for being so gracious," Thea said. She stressed the word *gracious* at a higher volume.

I stabbed a piece of cantaloupe with a fork. Adrenaline surged in me like I had one minute left in a spin class. Thea spread her napkin in her lap, smoothing it several times. Then she lifted a forkful of pasta salad to her mouth and raised her chin to the window, taking great interest in the hood of a Buick parked opposite our booth.

The truth hurts. Believe me, I've been on the receiving end of it enough to be able to teach a master class on the topic. Thea was clearly having a manic episode, or some kind of emotional breakdown, so I was justified in waving a flag in her face. She'd spent way more money than she had coming in. And the job market was so unpredictable.

She needed income; she needed health insurance. My God, what if she hurt herself moving into her house and had to have back surgery? Life was so precarious. She seemed oblivious to it all.

No, she was in denial. That's what it was. She was moving forward like everything was fine, like she'd won the lottery and was set for life.

"Did you win the lottery without telling me?" I asked. I tried to make it a joke.

Thea continued studying the Buick. She ate her pasta and pretended I wasn't there.

Okay, maybe I was rude. I've never done an intervention before. Was it wrong for me to worry about my best friend?

Lunch proceeded silently. I ate my flavorless sandwich and stared at my plate. How could I make her understand I had only her best interests at heart? As our plates emptied, our helpful waiter flew in to attend to our every need.

"Dessert, ladies? We have delicious cream cheese brownies, key lime pie that's to die for, and our famous lemon bars."

How he could claim that they were famous when no one beyond this neighborhood had ever heard of this place? That kind of imprecision drove me bananas with my freelancers. If he submitted that to me in writing, I'd mark it through with my bright red pen.

"I'll have a lemon bar," I said, because Thea had recommended them.

"Nothing for me," she said, smiling at the waiter and quickly turning back to the window. Was she one-upping me now in the appetite-control department? Was she retaliating by making me feel guilty about dessert? What was going on in that head of hers?

I tried to catch her eye, but she'd turned her body almost sideways. It was ridiculous. She didn't want to risk her eyes focusing on me, even by accident.

"Be right back with your lemon bar," the waiter said, whisking away our plates.

"Thea," I said, twisting my napkin in my fingers. "Please don't be angry with me. I'm looking out for you. Your house is wonderful. I'm terrified you'll run out of money before you find a new job. Aren't you…aren't you worried at all?"

"It's normal to be worried," she said. "But life happens. You can't stop enjoying yourself because bad things happen."

"No, but you also have to be reasonable. Prudent," I corrected myself. "You have to be prudent. This vacation—"

"I'm fine, Jane."

"But—"

"I'm fine," she insisted. "Maybe I really need this vacation."

"What if—"

"What if you stop mother-henning me? How many times must I tell you? It's none of your business. I'm an adult. I can look after myself. I don't need your unsolicited advice, not in person, not in written form. And more to the point, I don't want it. Quit bossing me around."

The waiter sailed in and slid a lemon bar under my trembling chin. "Our famous lemon bars," he sang. He turned to Thea. "Are you sure I can't tempt you with one?"

"No, thank you," she said.

"Coffee? Tea?"

Thea shook her head. I stared at the plate.

"Glass of wine?"

"Just the check, thanks," she said, a hard edge in her voice. "Separate ones."

"Very well, ladies," he said, and turned on his heel.

We paid the checks and stepped back out into the sunshine. The heat hit us like an oven door opening.

We trudged to Thea's house in silence. Back in her driveway, Thea jerked open the door of the moving truck. I followed. She wrenched the key in the ignition and shoved the truck into gear.

Miserable didn't adequately describe the ride back into the city. Thea kept the window rolled down, even though it was roasting, so that the wind made conversation impossible. She cranked up the volume on the radio, but neither of us sang along. The lemon bar, which tasted sour going down, weighed down my gut like a kettlebell.

We crossed over the Key Bridge into DC and traveled up Wisconsin Avenue. As we drew closer to the National Cathedral, I expected Thea to turn right and make our way toward her apartment; we loved to drive through the neighborhoods between the Cathedral and the zoo and look at the beautiful houses. But she kept going. When she finally turned right, on Nebraska, I knew exactly where we were going. Still, I hoped I was wrong.

"Do you need to fill up the truck?" I asked. "There's a gas station on the corner at Connecticut."

Thea shook her head. At the intersection at Connecticut Avenue, with the gas station on my right, she turned left. She was taking me home.

"Thanks for the help," Thea said as she pulled up outside my building.

"Thea, I'm sorry," I said as I opened the door. "I didn't mean to make you angry. I just worry about you."

"Well, try not to."

"Okay. I promise. But it won't be easy." I chuckled.

She didn't. She stared ahead, lips pressed tightly together.

"Well, maybe I'll see you later," I said, hopping out of the truck. I shut the door, then turned around to apologize one more time, but as I got to the window, she pulled away from me and merged with the traffic heading out of town.

CHAPTER SEVEN

Upstairs in my apartment, I peeled off my disgusting clothes and started the water in the shower. The image of the truck pulling away from me into traffic replayed in my mind like a bad syndicated TV series. It was on every channel; I couldn't shut it off. Thea never left without saying good-bye. Never.

I poured a glob of shampoo into my hand and smacked it into my wet hair. Why was she in such denial about her precarious situation? It wasn't like her to ignore a crisis. In fact, she was much more likely to seize upon it as a strategic opportunity. I'm the one who would freak out and try to hide under my bed; she'd be the one calming me down, giving me a step-by-step way to get out of my jam.

Stop mother-henning me. It's none of your business. Quit bossing me around.

I rinsed my hair and scrubbed myself all over. A sense

of dread had locked on to me, and I couldn't slough it off. Should I try again to discover how much cash she had in reserve or about her severance details? It was none of my business, true, but if I had more information, I could rest more easily.

I trusted Thea. I did. But seeing her willfully blind herself to reality scared me. It's almost like I had to be Thea because Thea was being me. We'd always stuck together. And she was acting exactly like I would. Flaky.

I got out of the shower and dried off. Usually I love taking long showers—I feel calmer afterward—but that afternoon I felt irritable. I watched TV and took out the trash, then I wandered from room to room, searching for something. My sense of perspective, maybe?

Why was Thea so angry with me? What was so wrong with what I did? She knew my heart was in the right place.

I decided to call Narin. She's only a few years older than me, but I've always thought of her more like an aunt than a big sister. Either she would set my head on straight or agree with me and we could vent together. I hoped it would be the latter.

When I called her, I could hear the sounds of her kids shrieking in the background.

"Jane! Lovely to hear from you. What have you been up to this baking-hot afternoon?"

"I've been helping Thea move. How about you?"

"We took the boys to the swimming pool, and I

thought they'd be exhausted by now, but no such luck. They're trying to give the dog a bath in the backyard, but the dog's not having it. They're mostly dumping soapy water on each other."

I couldn't decide if that sounded delightful or awful, but I didn't care. We'd had enough chitchat, right? If I didn't talk things through with Narin now, I'd burst.

"Did you know Thea's going on a two-week vacation to the Virgin Islands?" I asked.

"Yes," she said. "The lucky thing. Good for her. She needs some R & R."

Not the affirmation I was looking for. "But aren't you worried about her?"

"Why? Because she's going alone? She can look after herself. The Virgin Islands are safe. And besides, she'll be at a major resort. I'd be more afraid for her on the Metro late at night."

"No, I mean, aren't you worried about her finances? Taking an expensive vacation when she's lost her job and bought a house? It seems irresponsible."

"But she's been planning—" Narin began. She stopped abruptly.

"What? She's been planning what?"

"I see your point," she continued, "but Thea's a smart woman. She's wanted this house for too long to do anything stupid."

She was keeping something from me. She treated every confidence, even the most casual remarks, as if subject to attorney-client privilege. Her lips were more secure than Fort Knox. I sighed and picked at my fingernails, something I should stop doing but it's habit when I'm worried. "Maybe," I said.

Narin sighed. "Jane, I know your worry comes from a good place. But you've got to trust Thea."

"I do trust her. I just worry that she's having...I don't know... a stress-induced manic episode or something, and when she recovers from that shock she'll feel even worse because of the foolish things she's done."

"Perhaps. But neither of us is a psychologist. Even if it happened, why is it your job to save her?" I heard her snap her fingers. "Sami, no. Do not squirt your brother in the face with the hose."

"If it were me, I'd want you or her to stop me," I said. "What if she says, 'How could you let me do this?'"

"Well, what if she said that? What would that mean?"

"I don't know, financial ruin for her and permanent estrangement from my best friend for me?" What was her point?

"Unpleasant, for sure," she agreed, but I could tell she thought I was being irrational. On the coffee table, I spied an old stress toy, a little man with a vague snowman shape. I squeezed him hard and watched his head inflate. The poor guy looked like I felt, the membranes around his head stretched thin and starting to crack. I laid him gently back onto the table.

"Let's look at the other side," she continued. "I assume you've already told Thea how you feel. What will happen if you continue nagging her?"

"I don't know, Narin." This conversation felt like ones in high school, when the teacher kept pushing me to connect the dots. Couldn't she just tell me already?

"What's been the outcome so far?"

"Nothing. She doesn't listen to me," I said.

"Let's assume first that she's considering it privately. Give her the benefit of the doubt."

"Fine." The lawyer in her was building her case methodically to my jury of one.

"Let's assume she listened to you, but she's choosing other options. Isn't that her right?"

"Yes," I said. "But I don't like it."

"That's fair. Is it possible your advice is a voice in the back of her mind, warning her not to make additional irresponsible decisions?"

"Like what?"

"Like maxing out her credit card at IKEA buying stuff for her house. Or buying twenty pairs of new shoes at the Nordstrom sale. Or buying twenty pairs of shoes at Nordstrom when they're not on sale."

"All right." I could buy that theory. Thea dearly loved shopping. And with so much free time now, the malls and web boutiques would constantly tempt her. If it were me, I'd have to give my credit card to someone else for safekeeping.

"So that's one scenario," Narin said. "Here's another. Assume she listened to your advice, but she's annoyed that you're right. What would she do then?"

"She'd be angry with me. And she's stubborn. So she might be inclined to persist on her own path."

"Which would look like…?"

"She'd go on vacation, but she wouldn't enjoy it because she'd be angry I was right. And she'd kick herself for doing something dumb."

"Would she admit it to you?"

"No. Well, not right away. She'd deal with it on her own terms before she admitted it to me." Every fight we'd had in high school and college had ended this way. Those few fights we'd had when I was right, anyway.

"So she might be dealing with it now, in her own way."

"Yes," I said. This wasn't going to be one of those arguments I won.

"Is there any point in continuing to question her decisions?" Narin asked. "Emre? Emre, no. Let go of Rufus's tail."

"But she keeps making bad ones!" I said.

"Like what?"

I didn't want to admit to Narin that Thea'd thrown me out of our house-moving party. "I don't know," I said. "It's just a feeling I have."

"Jane, I get your concern. But your worry isn't founded on anything you can control."

"I can—"

"You can't." Her voice was firm but not unkind. It was the same tone that she used with her sons about the dog. "The more you tell her what to do, the more goodwill you revoke. Whatever's going on with her, she's not going to say, 'Jane, you're so right. Thank you for saving me from myself.'"

"At least, not now."

"Not now. If you persist, perhaps not ever."

"But if she—"

"Forgive me, but may I ask you a question?" Narin asked.

"What? Sure, I guess so."

"What are *you* most afraid of?"

The question made me feel uneasy, like I'd put on a jacket that was too tight and I couldn't unzip it or get out of the sleeves. "I'm not sure what you mean."

"I'm curious. Your anxiety is profound, I can tell. I wonder if something more is at work here? Is something else troubling you?"

The conversation had turned weird. You know when you've been caught in a lie, but your mom gives you a chance to redeem yourself and not make it worse? It felt like that, and it didn't make sense. I wasn't hiding anything.

"No," I said. "I only want my friend to be happy."

Narin didn't respond right away. I heard her boys in the background, laughing; water spraying hard against something hollow; the dog barking. Maybe she didn't hear me.

"Nothing's troubling me."

"Well, perhaps you're right, and it's nothing more," she said. "But you might think about that question this week. It's a question worthy of reflection. In fact, I ask it of myself all the time."

This conversation wasn't going anywhere. "Thanks, Narin," I said. "It sounds like things are nuts there with the boys, so I'll let you go. I appreciate your taking the time to hear me out."

"Any time, my dear. You're a good friend, Jane. But you can't save everyone."

"No, I know. I know." But that didn't mean I shouldn't try.

I didn't want to think about Narin's question. My stomach reminded me it was time for dinner, but nothing in the fridge looked appetizing.

I could order in from Jade Palace, I thought, but I ate Chinese last night. Would Delivery Guy see right through that? Probably; as should be clear by now, my flirtation game lacks a certain baseline finesse. But maybe he'd be flattered? He seemed interested last night. A little bit. Unless I was reading too much into it? Remembering his smile, my stomach did a somersault.

I caught a glimpse of myself in the hall mirror. While I was on the phone with Narin, my hair had air-dried, which meant it showed all the life and style of a jellyfish washed up on a beach. But I could fix that.

I went to the bathroom and dug in the cabinet under the sink for my old hot rollers. I wiped the dust off the old plastic cover, plugged them in to heat up, and opened my makeup bag. Shoot; I was out of mascara, and without it my eyes get lost in my face. Maybe a little extra eyeliner would compensate.

And what would I wear? My favorite black swing dress, which makes my legs look slim, lay slung over my bedroom chair. Not too wrinkled, though; nothing a little spritz of wrinkle releaser and a firm tug couldn't repair. The dress went perfectly with my cute red sandals, but the polish on my toenails was chipped. I could fix that, too.

Maybe I wouldn't have to resort to online dating after all. I pulled the sandals from the closet and turned around to grab the dress.

The bedroom looked storm-ravaged—Thea called my housekeeping style "Hurricane Jane"—and to be honest, I'd need to clean up the whole apartment, not just the bedroom. I didn't want him seeing how I really lived. But that was a day-long project, at least. Maybe I could throw everything into the shower and pull the curtain?

The mingled scents of hot dust and plastic signaled that the aged hot rollers were ready for action. I went in and lifted the cover on the set, but as I looked in the mirror to roll the first lock of hair, I paused.

For heaven's sake, what was the matter with me? Who puts *any* effort in to getting a Chinese food delivery?

I rolled my eyes and shook my head at my reflection. Then I unplugged the rollers, threw my hair into a pony-tail, and went down the street to the deli for a meatball sub. Maybe a little heavy for a ninety-five-degree day, but my insides needed a hug. On the way back I nipped into the drugstore for a new mascara, plus some chocolate and trashy magazines for fun.

In the lobby of my building, I saw a neighbor, Mrs. Nuñez, stepping into the elevator with her kids, Dina and Rafael.

"Mrs. Nuñez? Hold the elevator!"

She stuck her head out and smiled as she held the door open for me. I sprinted to the elevator, where the kids were jostling to push the button. "Hello, Jane," she said. "Aren't you going out on this lovely Saturday night?"

"No, I'm staying in."

Dina punched the button for the fifth floor as Rafael peeked into my take-out bag. "That smells awesome," he said.

"Meatball sub," I said. He licked his lips.

"A young woman like you needs to go out on a weekend night," Mrs. Nuñez said. "Don't you have a boyfriend?"

"No."

"You're not going to find one sitting in your apartment," she pointed out.

The elevator rivaled the one at my office for efficiency. The light above the door dragged from 2 to 3.

"Actually, I met someone earlier this week," I said. "Unfortunately, he's got to work tonight." At least part of that statement was true. It might all be true. Just because I didn't know didn't make it false.

She wiggled her eyebrows at me. "Oooh-ooh," Rafael sang, dancing around in the elevator. "Jane's got a boyfriend, Jane's got a boyfriend." Dina raised her hands to her throat and made gagging sounds. Her mother gave her a playful shove.

"Stop it," she said. "Just you wait five or six more years. We'll see who thinks boys are so gross then."

Dina wrinkled her nose in disgust.

"I don't know, Dina. You might be on to something," I said. The doors slid open at last, and the kids bolted out.

"Well, have a good evening," Mrs. Nuñez said as we both stepped out of the elevator. "I hope it works out with your new friend. A nice girl like you needs to settle down."

The grimace rose to my face like a reflex. "Yep, my mom reminds me every time I talk to her. Good night!" I shoved the key in the door and flung myself inside, bolting the lock behind me.

I flicked on the television for some company, grabbed a soda from the fridge, and sat down on the sofa with my sandwich and magazines. Where to start? "Legs for Days!" promised *Elle*. "Eat a Giant Lunch, Drop 5 Pounds in a Month" swore a publication allegedly devoted to *Women's Health*. "Love Your Body!" *Cosmopolitan* commanded from a headline papered over the trim waistline of a cover model with the tightest bod I've seen this side of Barbie. Beneath the headline, in finer print: "Tone Every Zone in Just Minutes a Day!" You know, in case I was confused about expectations.

Why, again, had I picked these up? The editors would surely not approve of my meatball sub, I thought as I sank my teeth into it. The bun sagged with sauce, but the cheese glued it all together long enough to make the journey from the wrapper to my face. Aromas of oregano and fennel bewitched my nostrils. I swallowed, feeling the heat slide down my throat into my stomach. I kicked the magazines under the coffee table.

Screw advice. If it meant I couldn't enjoy a meatball sub, who needed it?

I finished the sub and fished in the bag for my chocolate. Out the corner of my eye, another periodical peeked from beneath the coffee table. "It's Not Too Late to Get a Bikini Butt."

I shouldn't get too invested in Delivery Guy; after all, I didn't even know his name. Furthermore, I didn't want to hear what Mom would have to say about him: "A delivery man? Don't you think you should aim a little higher? You can't raise a family on that salary." Never mind the abuse she'd give me about putting her grandchildren in daycare and going back to work. Grandkids that didn't even exist.

Still, the image of Delivery Guy kept elbowing its way into my mind. Experience told me not to get too excited about him. Unfortunately for me, I seldom listened to Experience.

CHAPTER EIGHT

O n the way to work on Monday, I decided the conversation with Narin had helped. The part about how Thea might be responding, I mean. Something about the way Narin talks relaxes me. Unfortunately, Narin doesn't live in my head. She lives with her husband and two little kids, so she has more important things to do than babysit an adult woman.

Later that day, Keith dropped in for a chat.

"Hey, Desmond," he said, making himself comfortable in my guest chair.

"Hey, Keith," I said without looking away from my screen.

He sat there, tapping his fingers on his knees. I composed an email to my regular freelancers, requesting feature ideas for the coming issues. I updated the events calendar for the next issue. Then I emailed our major advertisers, asking for updates to their ads.

Keith didn't budge.

"Can I help you with something?" I asked, slamming the keyboard back in its drawer and giving him what I hoped was a clear I-don't-have-time-for-conversation glare.

He bit his thumbnail. "So, um. Yeah." His eyes rested on the bookshelf above my desk. "Let's get a drink after work," he told the shelf.

"Sorry, Keith. I have plans," I lied.

"Okay, tomorrow then," he urged the shelf.

"Nope. Plans then, too."

"Name the day," he said.

"Keith," I said.

He turned his eyes to me, finally, and gave me a tight-lipped smile. "I'm not going to take no for an answer."

"I think you're going to have to. Now, if you'll excuse me, I have work to tend to."

He wiggled in the chair, as if building a nest for himself. "I'm not leaving until you say yes."

"Keith, get out. I have a phone call to make."

"I'll wait."

"No, get out."

"Promise me you'll go out for a drink with me this week. Then I'll go."

Why couldn't he take a hint? What did it say about me, that I couldn't get rid of this guy?

Whatever. Anything to get rid of him now; I'd deal with the consequences later. "Fine, Keith. You win. Now leave. I have work to do."

He grinned and rose from his chair, pumping his fist.

Should I be flattered that he felt so excited to have extracted a promise from me? Why couldn't Delivery Guy—or *anyone* else on earth—act the same way? One man's trophy was another's consolation prize. I slammed the door behind him as he left.

The staffs of all the construction magazines met that afternoon for their monthly strategy session. Keith sat opposite me at the conference table, staring the entire time.

Sarah, the intern, nudged me. "Keith won't stop staring at you."

"I know," I muttered.

"It's creepy," she pointed out. "Aren't you bothered?"

"Yes."

"You should do something about him."

I should. But confrontation was even more unpleasant than hiding in the women's bathroom until he left for the day. Maybe he would get hit by a bus after work and I wouldn't have to deal with it. Or maybe Thea's boyfriend would have found someone to set me up with. Crap! Why didn't I think to tell him I'd met someone? I smacked my forehead with the heel of my hand. So, so obvious. Once again, the ideal excuse had evaded me in time of need. No worry. Whenever he brought it up to me again—and no doubt, it would be sooner than I wanted—I'd have a story for him.

I raised my eyes from the notepad where I'd been doodling. Keith's eyes met mine.

"What is it?" he mouthed at me. "What's wrong?"

I turned to the head of the table, where Rita was drawing a pie chart on a whiteboard.

A pen shot across the table and stabbed me in the hand.

"Ow," I said. Rita turned around.

"Are you all right?"

"I'm fine," I said, rubbing my hand. When she turned back to the whiteboard, I glared at Keith. "What the f—" I mouthed, biting my lip on the last word.

"Sorry," he mouthed back, his face all concern and sweetness. "I'm worried about you." His unibrow plunged in the middle, a vague V of sympathy.

Next to me, Sarah stifled a snort. I passed her the tissue box.

I gave Keith the slip that afternoon by taking the stairs down. Nine flights, but even in heels it was better than being trapped in a slow-moving elevator with him. My mom called as I hit the pavement outside, but I sent her to voicemail. I could imagine her response if I complained about Keith: "Well, honey, at least he's interested. Why don't you have that drink with him? He might not be as bad as all that."

The woman seated next to me on the train was reading an article, "How to Get a Guy to Like You." I closed my eyes. Those articles never have any useful information, like, say, how to reconcile their advice with the basic need to feel good about yourself.

I glanced at my phone. Mom didn't leave a voicemail. Just as I settled back in my seat to relax, the email notification popped up. Of course.

"Dear Jane, Paul Alexander is moving to DC next month. I told him you would call him and show him around town. His cell number is 804-555-0176. Call him now and make plans while you're thinking about it.

Love, Mom."

———

Thea called me on Tuesday, asking if I'd take care of her cat while she was gone.

"Of course," I said. "So. How's everything going with the move?"

"It's good."

"You're not going to believe what happened at work yesterday. Keith came and parked himself in my office and would not leave until I promised to have a drink with him. Can you imagine?"

"What did you do?"

"I said I would, only to get him out. He was like a child having a tantrum. I didn't want to risk a blowup or anything embarrassing. I just wanted him out of the office."

"That's hardly going to put a stop to him," Thea pointed out.

I bit my lip. "Yeah." I told her how creepy Keith was during the editorial meeting, acting all mushy and concerned about me. "Like now he thinks I'm his girl-friend or something."

Thea heaved a sigh at me. "Do you see my point? If you seriously don't like it, you have to put a stop to it. Being evasive is only leading him on. You have to put your foot down."

"But I—"

"You should talk to HR. Lodge a complaint."

"HR?" I asked. "Eww. But then they'll call us both in,

probably, and mediate a conversation, and—"

"And put a stop to it."

"I don't know. It might not work. I'd rather limit any conversation I have to have with him at all. Having a mediated confrontation? Inviting some spectator from HR to witness it all? That sounds so icky."

"Is it as icky as his advances? Get over it. You have to stop it, 'cause he's not going to. And seriously. What he's doing? It's sexual harassment. Refusing to leave your office until you agree to go out with him? That's not acceptable."

"He's just pathetic. I don't want to be bitchy."

"Pathetic or not, he seems to think that holding you hostage in your own office is acceptable behavior. Forget about about being bitchy, you need to stand up for yourself. You don't stand up to him now, you don't know what he might do next."

Could Keith do something worse? It was hard to picture him—ugh, I didn't want to picture anything, except him being the target of an alien abduction and disappearing from Earth.

"Well," I said.

"Well."

"Say, speaking of having a drink, did you ask Richard if he knew anyone he could set me up with?"

"I broke up with Richard. You're on your own there."

"Oh! Yay, you." She knew I didn't like him. "How do you feel?"

"I feel great."

"That's wonderful. Who needs men, right?"

"I need to go. I gotta finish packing."

"Sure, sure. I'll take care of Cleo for you."

"I'll leave a key for you with the rental office," she said. I could her her rustling something in the background; she had already moved on to other things.

"Have a safe trip," I said.

But Thea had already hung up.

CHAPTER NINE

I spent Wednesday, the day Thea left for vacation, playing hide-and-seek from Keith. Working in the ladies' bathroom and not having Thea to kvetch to only reinforced her commandment to get HR involved. But every time I thought about filing a complaint, I felt the urge to bolt into a stall and retch. They'd probably just laugh at me, say I was being hypersensitive, he's a wimp, get over it. Not only would I not stop Keith, I'd humiliate myself as well. What were they going to do, put a restraining order on him? "You shall not walk within fifty feet of Jane Desmond's office?" I couldn't win, could I?

Instead, I called in sick on Thursday morning and went by Thea's apartment to feed Cleo. The apartment was mostly empty, and Cleo ran wildly around the vacant rooms. She bumped her head against my leg as I scraped a can of wet food into her bowl. When she settled in to feast, I sifted out the litter box.

When Thea came back two weeks from now, she

wouldn't need the remaining week on her lease to finish cleaning out her apartment before she moved for good. Her bed was gone; she was sleeping on a camping cot in her sleeping bag. Clothes lay folded in piles on the floor— T-shirts, shorts, socks, underwear. A milk crate next to her cot held a clip light. It was like she'd regressed back to being a college student, or maybe she took too many interior design directions from me.

In the crate-cum-nightstand sat some folders and manila envelopes.

I did not invade her stuff. I happened to notice one of the folders was from her old office; a sticker on the front showed the company's logo. The one closest to me was definitely her severance packet. Someone from an outplacement-services firm had stapled a business card to the front.

But I pledged to trust her. I turned on my heel, gave Cleo a pat, and ran out the door, locking it behind me before I could change my mind.

I got all the way downstairs and outside the building before the thought occurred to me: She's gone for two whole weeks, which is a lot of time to be absent from the job search. What if I helped her out, just a little? Not by looking at her severance and making a budget for her, nothing like that. But maybe I could let her network know she was looking? I mean, job searches took forever, didn't they?

I let myself back into the apartment and went to the bedroom. Cleo lay in front of the crate. She glared at me.

I knew I should get out of there; my anxiety and my conscience were grappling like the characters in those

WWF matches my high school friends used to watch. If Thea went looking in my severance details, even if it was well-intended, I'd feel betrayed. I'd feel naked. We might be as close as sisters, but still, we don't get naked in front of each other. You know what I mean.

"I'm not going to look at the money," I told Cleo. "That's none of my business. I'm just going to help her network. She told me I could do that."

Cleo rolled over on her back.

Just to prove my point, I picked up the severance folder and shoved it to the back of the stack of things in the crate, behind textbooks for French and art history. What were those doing in there? She'd never taken those courses in college. A syllabus stuck in the front of the French book showed the course was current. Intensive French 3. What on earth was that about?

Her resume, which is what I'd hoped to find, now stood in the front of the stack. Someone had marked up a printout with comments. She must have gone to the outplacement-services people. Good for her! But why hadn't she told me?

She was, in fact, taking steps in the right direction. What she needed from me, more than anything, would be cooperation. Doing things in her service. I'd said I'd help her do the icky business of networking, getting her information out there. She'd even said it would be helpful. She'd *agreed*.

I refreshed Cleo's water bowl and gave her a final see-you-later pat. Then I took the copies of the resume with me and locked the door.

I walked slowly past Jade Palace, craning my neck to

look inside, but I didn't see Delivery Guy. I crossed over Connecticut Avenue and waited for the bus to take me home.

At home, I turned on my computer and pulled up Microsoft Word. I typed up Thea's resume, formatting it in serious, professional, 12 point Times New Roman. I made all the changes the outplacement people suggested. Then I tweaked the formatting, making sure the page broke on the end of a paragraph, and I proofread it backward twice. Finally I saved it as a PDF and opened my browser.

Thea used four passwords. She couldn't keep track of more, so she cycled through them on her different profiles and accounts. She's told me each of them at various times, because sometimes she wanted me to do her posting for her. You know, like you might tell your sister.

First stop: LinkedIn. I guessed this password on the first try (CleoCat2010) and updated her profile to match the changes the outplacement people made.

For example, they recommended she change her job title so it described her work product (God, what a term!) and personal mission statement. Thea scribbled two sample ones on the back of her marked-up resume:

"Thea Willis is an efficient and motivated health insurance industry professional with deep experience leading teams focused on quality customer care."

"Thea Willis is a health insurance industry professional highly skilled in team building and customer-focused service provision."

I liked the second one better, so I posted that as her mission statement.

I copied and pasted the updated work experience into her profile. Then the site prompted me to list volunteer work and special interests and skills, as she hadn't yet listed any. Fortunately, I knew Thea's interests like the back of my hand. She volunteered with the local no-kill animal shelter and tutored at a nearby elementary school. Special interests and skills? Apparently she'd enrolled in a French class; I might as well put that down. I listed her proficiency as twenty percent, which was both arbitrary and probably a stretch at this point but at least it demonstrated her commitment to lifelong learning.

I looked at the companies she followed; there were jobs open at three of them. I couldn't tell even from her resume whether they matched her skills or not. How did resume writing become an exercise in obfuscation and nonsense? I submitted her resume to their HR departments anyway; what harm could it do? The last thing HR wanted to do was read anyone's resume.

I took screen shots of the job listings so she could refer to them when the time came.

I was feeling good, on a roll. How else could I be of service?

Right, networking! I sent a message to all her first-line contacts. I kept it short and to the point:

Dear Friends and Colleagues,

I'm writing to let you know I'm seeking new employment opportunities. I'm open to full-time and/or contract work. If you know of any opportunities opening up where you work, or hear of suitable positions through the grapevine, I'd be grateful if you passed the information on to me.

Best regards,
Thea

Next stop: Facebook. It took two tries to guess this password (slightly harder, because I forgot she added an exclamation mark: GoTerps!2004).

I scribbled a status update, but before I posted it I paused. First of all, Thea might update her Facebook from her vacation, and I didn't want those messages superseding the work status notification. It wouldn't look good for her if she posted photos of herself on the beach when she should be looking for work. Instead, I made a small mailing group of some of her closest friends in the area and sent a tweaked version of the LinkedIn message:

Hi, Friends,

As you might have heard, Janus downsized their claims processing department. I'm on vacation for a short while, but as soon as I get back I'll be fired up to look for new employment. I'll be looking for full-time work in the DC area, but contract work would be okay as well. If you know of anything opening up, please message me privately. Here's my LinkedIn profile, where you can read more about my work experience and skills: http://linkedin.com/profile/TheaWillis20170708

Thanks in advance for any leads.

Best,

Thea

A much better decision on my part. Any information she received would not appear on her wall. It might give her a slight advantage over any unemployed former work colleagues who might also be her Facebook friends. I'd set things in motion; she could amplify the message when she got back.

And finally, her email (CleoCat2010 again). I took care this time not to send messages to folks who'd gotten Facebook or LinkedIn notifications. I scrolled through her address book, stunned by the number of contacts. I selected twenty people who I felt sure had local connections. Twenty isn't that many, certainly as a percentage of her total network. I had to leave her something to do.

I copied and pasted the Facebook message and attached the PDF of the resume, so people could forward it or print it out if they're old fashioned like that.

Your Message Has Been Sent.

There. Just a nudge to get her some momentum. She'd get responses in no time at all—who wouldn't jump at the chance to hire Thea?—and that would surely temper any irritation she felt toward me at having pushed her into the deep end of the job-hunting pool.

Before I could log out, replies came in. Two said sorry, nothing available at their workplaces but they'd keep their ears open, which was nice. Two more said that there might be positions opening up in the next six months and they'd pass on info as they got it. And one actually said she heard a manager was leaving and it would be a good fit for her. Amazing!

I clicked "Reply" and scribbled off: "Great news! Thanks so much. Do you have a job posting? Who's hiring for the position? Please send their email so I can send my info." My mouse flew to the "Send" button.

Something made me pause. I couldn't imagine her not wanting to pursue the job, but what if, by chance, she didn't want it? I didn't want to burn any bridges on her behalf.

But the clock was ticking; it's always ticking. What if someone else snatched up the job before she had a chance to respond?

My hand drifted to my mouth, and I nibbled on my thumbnail. What would Thea do? When faced with an important decision, she weighed the pros and cons. So I grabbed and envelope and started a list:

Pros:

- Managerial job (step up).
- Likely pay increase.
- Easy commute, on her new Metro line.

Cons:

- I don't know how best to present her.
- What did she actually *do*? Can't sell her strengths.
- ~~Not my job to pursue?~~

The pros clearly outweighed the cons, so I hit "Send."

Furthermore, it was a truth universally acknowledged that the last thing HR departments wanted to do was hire someone. That's why they were chronically slow. And yet they were as unavoidable as a yeast infection after a week spent wearing yoga pants. I could take on that drudgery for her, fill out her HR application and let her do the important work of sending her information to the hiring manager.

The email came back almost instantly:

"Here's the HR application link. The job is a managerial position here at Kaiser. Let me check who the hiring manager is and get back to you. Good luck! Would love to work with you."

I clicked on the online application form, just to look. It was a simple thing, requesting only basic contact information and an attached resume. It did have space for a cover letter.

I bit off part of my thumbnail and threw the piece into the trash. What would Thea want me to do?

I twisted in my chair. To be honest, she'd want to do it herself. And I'd feel terrible if I wrote a bad letter and kept her from getting the interview.

I scanned the form. It seemed I could fill it out and save it for her to complete later. I scribbled in basic details.

My stomach reminded me it was time for lunch, so I got up to fix myself a sandwich. I cracked open a soda from the fridge, took a long swallow, and set it down on the table next to the computer. Then I went back to retrieve the sandwich and some chips. As I set down the plate, I knocked over a pile of mail I hadn't yet dealt with, sending it spilling to the floor. The pile took out my mouse, which plunged over the table's edge like a cliff diver.

"Gwraaar," I growled, searching for the mouse amongst the fallen envelopes. As I picked up a sheaf of the mail, I heard a clicking sound. It sounded like a lock clicking, on a gate you can't go back through.

"No," I said. "No. No no no no no!" I turned back to the laptop screen. The application was gone. In its place was a message:

Thank you. Your application has been received.

Gaaaaaa! Now what? I hit the Back button but that didn't help. It was gone, and I couldn't retrieve it.

My stomach jounced like people were playing the Olympic handball gold medal match in there. I ran to the bathroom and locked myself in.

Okay, okay. Calm down. Think it through.

I know, right now, that I had no business doing any of this. I had no business going into Thea's accounts, no business starting that job application on her behalf. If I could rewind the clock, I would. I will definitely not do anything like this going forward.

However, I don't think I wrote anything unprofessional on the application. Or anything incorrect. I am ninety percent sure I didn't put anything in the cover letter box. Did I?

I was pretty sure I didn't. And that meant it was going to be okay, because it wasn't harmful. At worst, it was benign. Right? I didn't show her to best advantage, true, but I didn't have to do damage control. Did I?

Calm down, Jane. Mountain ranges formed in less time than it took HR to sort resumes. That's why I even thought about doing it in the first place. They'd probably have thousands of applications for this position, demanding weeks' worth of review, before they'd get to Thea's application. By that time Thea would have come back already, contacted the hiring manager, and sent in all her papers. HR would be like, yeah, whatever, when the hiring person wanted to set up an interview. They wouldn't think twice about her application not having a cover letter. It'd be one more thing they didn't have to read. I'd actually saved them work.

To be honest, I didn't buy that last thought, but pretending I did gave me the courage to look in the bathroom mirror.

"It's going to be okay," I said to myself. I didn't look reassured.

I repeated those words to myself back down the hall and into my kitchen. I repeated them as I logged out of Thea's account as fast as I could and as I restarted my computer for good measure. I repeated them as I threw all of my old mail into the recycling bin, washed my dishes, and put them away. I repeated them that afternoon at the gym, that evening as I fixed dinner, and that night before I turned out the light.

On Friday, Keith was hanging out by my door when I got to work. He looked nicer than normal, which is to say he'd tucked in his currently stain-free shirt.

"So, Desmond. I've been thinking about where to go tonight for our drink."

"I can't go tonight, Keith."

"What? You promised." He stepped aside to let me open my office door, then followed me inside.

"Keith, get out, please."

"No!" he whined. "You promised. You promised you'd go for a drink with me."

I slapped my briefcase on my desk. "I didn't promise *when*."

Clenching his jaw, he planted himself in my chair.

"Oh, no. Don't get comfortable. You're not staying."

"You promised you'd go for a drink. I'm staying here until we have a firm date on the calendar. Day, time, and place." He crossed his arms and glared at me.

"You're acting like a child. Get out of my office."

He shook his head.

I couldn't believe it. He was going to sit here and pout until I made an actual date with him. I walked over to his chair, grabbed its arm, and gave it a pull.

Of course it wouldn't budge. "What are you doing?" he asked.

I'd had the idea to drag him out into the hall and lock the door behind me, but I couldn't shift the chair. Crap, maybe Thea was right. Maybe HR was the only way to deal with this.

"Fine," I said, releasing the chair, straightening up, and smoothing the wrinkles from my trousers. "I'm sick of this. You can't hold me hostage in here. I'm taking this up with HR."

"What?!"

But I was already out the door and down the hall.

"Desmond! Wait!" he called. I pretended not to hear him.

HR was one floor down and in the opposite corner of the building. Rather than take the chance he might catch up with me at the elevator, I bolted for the stairs and sprinted in my heels to the HR manager's office. I knocked before I realized I was completely out of breath and must look like a lunatic.

Barbara Klingman, certified HR professional, opened the door. "Good morning," she said, her painted-on eyebrows knitting together as soon as she saw me panting and gripping the cubicle wall opposite her. "Can I help you?"

I nodded. She beckoned me into her office and closed the door.

"Have a seat," she said, gesturing to her guest chair. Her desk looked like an adoption center for tiny ceramic cat figurines. She must have had two dozen of them.

"Nice cats," I said, stalling for time.

"Thank you." She stroked one fondly. "They're my passion. Now, what can I do for you today?"

Barbara Klingman folded her hands on her desk, relaxed her eyebrows, and smiled at me, like a kindergarten teacher coaxing the alphabet out of a shy child. Her frosted blond hair was sprayed into a tight helmet. She looked a bit like my aunt Betty, another woman in my life desperate to see me settled down.

"I…"

She waited patiently. It's an old trick to make people talk. The longer you let the silence build, the more uncomfortable it gets, and the more compelled a person feels to fill the space. In my case, it gave me time to think.

Did I really want to do this? Lodge a formal complaint? What would my coworkers think? I couldn't expect to keep it confidential, not really. Keith would probably blow my cover, complaining to everyone he spoke to that I'd run to HR to get out of having a drink with him, like I'd promised I'd do. It was bad enough that most of the office had to witness Keith's unabashed pursuit of me on a daily basis. Did they have to be spectators to our personnel dispute as well?

Barbara Klingman waited.

Still, Thea was probably right. If I didn't complain to HR, he'd pull this again. He clearly had no qualms about camping out in my office to get his way. Cliff, my direct supervisor, might let me work from home once a week if I had a good reason, but if he got wind that it was only to get away from an annoying coworker, he'd never agree. As usual, Thea was right. I had to stop it.

"I'm having a problem with a coworker," I said.

She nodded. "Go on."

"His name is Keith, he works on *Cement World*, and he keeps asking me out. I've made excuses not to, but he won't take a hint. On Monday he wouldn't leave my office until I agreed to have a drink with him. I said yes, just to get him out, but I didn't say when. Now it's Friday and he thinks today's the day, but when I said no, he had a tantrum and parked himself in my guest chair and wouldn't leave."

"I see," she said.

"I can't work like this," I said, feeling stupid for pointing out the obvious.

"Nor should you have to," she said.

Well. That was easier than I'd expected. Maybe she'd call Keith in, give him that restraining order, and I'd never have to talk to him again. I straightened up in my chair and smiled.

"Now, we do have a protocol to follow in cases like this," Barbara said, turning around to her bookshelf and extracting a thick binder. She leafed through the pages, her long, bubblegum-pink fingernail tracing the paragraphs until she found what she sought. "Aha. Here we are. So, the first step in this process is to have a mediated conversation. You and Keith will meet with me and another HR colleague, and you will explain why this behavior bothers you and what your expectations are. He will have a chance to respond. If the behavior does not change, we will then escalate to step two."

"Which is?"

"A verbal reprimand and notification of his supervisor."

"A verbal reprimand? That's all?" I couldn't believe it. "That's nothing. He's not going to pay attention to that. I just ordered him out of my office, and he clamped himself into my chair like he was going to blast off on a rocket. I told him to get out, that I couldn't work like this. If that's not a reprimand, if that's not setting my expectations clearly, then what is?"

"We have a formal process to follow," Barbara Klingman said. "It's important to follow these steps to secure redress on your behalf."

"To reiterate what I've already done?"

"Yes. It may not seem like much, but it makes a difference, having HR involved and documenting the process. And notification of the supervisor. That usually helps."

Maybe usually, but it wouldn't in this case. Keith's supervisor used his business trips to explore the regional variations in "gentleman's clubs." I didn't see any natural allies emerging from his department.

"You know Ken Drummond's a creep and a lech, right?"

Barbara Klingman's lips pushed together into a thin wrinkle. "Miss Desmond—"

"Never mind, forget it," I said, standing up. "This process isn't going to get me anywhere. I don't want to have to retrace the steps I've already taken with even more people watching. Can't you call him in privately and tell him if he does it again, he's fired?"

"No, I can't. That wouldn't be fair to the accused."

"What about fair to me? I'm the one who has to deal with his garbage."

"Do you want to initiate the process, or not?"

"Is there any point?"

"You'll have to decide for yourself," she said. "The process is in place for a reason. Both sides have to be considered. The process establishes the facts. And then—"

"I'm sorry to have bothered you," I said, rolling my eyes. "I should have known this wouldn't solve anything. I'll just keep hiding from him. Forget I was even here. I've got to get back to work."

CHAPTER TEN

A weekend should be a time of recreation, but on Friday evening thoughts of Thea's accidental application crept back to my mind like mildew in the shower and wouldn't let me rest. I knew I'd screwed up; the question was, what to do about it? Should I leave it alone, trusting the company's hiring staff to lose her application? Or should I log back in to her account and withdraw it? The more I considered the options, the more confused I got. Who knows what Thea might have discovered while on vacation, checking her emails and her accounts. Was she boiling mad at me from sixteen hundred miles away? And beyond the obvious breach of Thea's trust, a nagging fear had latched on to me, whispering in my ear that I'd done something slightly on the wrong side of the law.

Once again, I needed Narin's advice. As an attorney, wise counsel is her stock in trade. That, and getting people out of trouble. It was a good thing she was my friend, because she charged a billion dollars an hour and I couldn't afford her for real.

"Narin? It's Jane."

"Hi, Jane. How are you?" Her voice was rushed.

"I'm good," I said. "Are you busy? You sound busy."

She sighed. "I am busy, but then I'm always busy. I have time to talk. What's up?"

"Are you sure? Because I can wait."

"I'm sure."

I took a deep breath. She was my friend; she'd be on my side. I needed to do this in one move, like ripping off a bandage.

"I need your advice. I think I might have done something…not *illegal*, exactly—"

"Hold on. 'Not illegal, exactly'? Are you asking me for legal advice, or friendly advice?"

"Um, I don't know." Which wasn't true; I wanted free legal advice.

"Because if it's a legal matter, you shouldn't say anything because I could be compelled in court to reveal what you tell me—except if you hire me."

"Hire you? I can't afford you, Narin."

She sighed. I could practically hear her rubbing her temples in anticipation of a Jane-flavored headache. "Promise you'll give me a dollar in exchange for being your attorney on this issue."

"Okay, that's a deal."

"All right. Now, you were saying…"

I gulped. Okay. I took another deep breath. "You know I've been worrying about Thea and her job? So, she's on vacation, and I might have accidentally applied for a job on her behalf and now I'm worried because the application might not be that professional and I don't want to hurt her chances and she's going be furious with me so what should I do?" There! I did it.

"Just a moment," Narin said. Through the phone, I heard a drawer open and shut. Paper rustled, a pen clicked.

When a lawyer starts taking notes during your conversation, be advised that what you've done is not nothing. It's definitely something.

"You did *what* while she's on vacation?"

I took another deep breath. "I accidentally applied for a job for her."

"How do you—"

"I *know*, I know I shouldn't have done it, and I feel really bad. She's going to be furious at me and rightfully so. But I'm freaking out! What if she's getting responses right now and when she logs in to her email and reads them she's like, 'What the hell is this?' I was only trying to help, I swear it. What should I do?"

"Tell me the whole story, from the beginning," Narin instructed. "Don't leave anything out, and don't lie. I can't help you if you don't tell me the whole truth."

Oh my God, I'd committed a felony. Maybe she'd defend me *pro bono*. Except she did some kind of contract work, not criminal defense. "Am I going to jail?"

"No one is sending you to jail." I could practically hear her eyes roll through the phone. "But my God, Jane, you really had no business doing this."

"I know! I know! I just got carried away. It's not like I killed someone, though. I was trying to do a good thing." I pulled a rubber band from the kitchen drawer, stretching it to give my hands something to do. It snapped and stung me on the hand, raising a red welt. Jeez, even my household supplies turned against me.

"Begin at the beginning."

I gave her the background, which she mostly knew anyway, about how panicked I was to see Thea acting like I would, directionless and unmotivated. "So I was in this heightened state of worry already, and then she had me come over and help her move. I got to see the house and when I got inside I saw how perfect it was for her. When we went to lunch, she told me about her plan to go on vacation for two weeks at a luxury resort. And I panicked…I think she's having a nervous breakdown."

"I see," Narin said, in a way that I couldn't interpret at all.

"What does that mean?"

"I mean, I am following you. Go on."

I wanted to argue with her, but when Narin tells you in her lawyer voice to do something, you obey. "And then we talked, and you put my mind at ease. Do you remember?"

"I do," she said. "I thought you were going to trust her."

"I was. But then I got an idea of something simple I could do for her, just to get the ball rolling. While I was feeding Cleo I saw her resume. It had been marked up by the outplacement firm her company hired. And I thought, I could type it up for her and post it, and let people know that she's looking. And that would be *helpful*, because it would put her friends on the lookout for her while she's away. Like delegating the job search to her *friends*."

"Oh, dear," Narin said.

"I cleaned up her resume and posted it on LinkedIn, and sent it to some of her email and Facebook contacts."

"How did you get into her accounts?"

"I know her passwords. She only has four."

"Jane, that's a serious breach—"

"She's had me log in to her accounts before, and I thought I would do her a favor. You're supposed to be listening to my case, right?"

Narin huffed. "Fine. Carry on."

"That was yesterday. I promised myself I'd only do this one thing, and then I'd leave it alone until Thea got back. But I got a response instantly about an open managerial position, that the friend said would be a perfect fit for her. So I requested the listing—"

"Oh, Jane. No."

"Wait. I asked for the listing so Thea could have all the details to apply for the job herself."

"It's still a breach—"

"I'm not finished." I was desperate to confess the whole thing; I couldn't spill it fast enough. "So they sent me the listing, and there was a link to the application form. All it wanted was her contact information and the resume. I filled all that out. There was a space for a cover letter, but I absolutely did not write a cover letter."

"Okay…"

"Then, while I had it open, I got hungry, so I went to fix a sandwich. And I had a little accident, and the mouse button got clicked. So the application got submitted by accident. *Accident*," I said, like Narin might not have heard me the first two times.

Narin sighed, the same exasperated sigh my mom used to heave at me when I was a teenager. Any second now she'd tell me how disappointed she was in me. I wouldn't have been surprised if she sent me to my room to think about what I'd done. I would have gone, too.

Instead of a lecture, I got an explosion. "Why is it your responsibility to find her a job?" Narin demanded. "I don't understand why you would do this. You know she's got her new business to—"

"What? New business? What new business?"

"Sh—. Ugh! Nothing, forget I said anything."

"No, not nothing. What are you talking about?" Thea was planning to start a new business? Why didn't she tell me?

"I forgot you didn't know. I shouldn't tell you this. Thea specifically asked me not to. But given what you've done—"

"She specifically asked you not to tell me something? Are you sure? Are you sure you didn't misunderstand her?"

"I am quite sure. Thea is leaving the insurance business altogether. She's starting her own business, and she's been planning it for months. She hadn't planned to launch it just yet, not when she'd just closed on the house, but given the downsizing she's moving ahead with her plan."

My jaw dropped. "But...that's amazing. That's wonderful. Why didn't she tell me?"

"Look, I've said far too much."

I stood there, listening to arcade-type music drifting in the background behind her. Her boys must be playing video games.

She was waiting for me, but I didn't know what she wanted me to say. I made a guess.

"So what should I do? Should I call the company and—"

"NO!" Narin said. "For the love of God, Jane. Stop. Just stop. You have done enough damage already. My God, your instincts are unbelievable."

It's one thing to tell yourself you've done harm, but to hear it from someone else, someone you respect, was so damning. My eyes got hot; I had to blink fast to make them stop stinging.

"Narin, I'm sorry. I wish I'd never done it. Am I in serious trouble? Or let me put that another way. Exactly how deep is the trouble I am in? Like, knee deep?" I said hopefully.

"Not knee deep," she said. "You are in way, way over your head."

My mouth dropped open, and my stomach felt like it was going to climb out and make a run for it. "Have I... have I committed fraud or something? Was that identity theft? Or wire fraud or one of those kinds of crimes? You... you wouldn't seriously file charges against me, would you?" I sat down in my chair. My hands were shaking. "I never thought—oh God! Narin, PLEASE tell me you're not going to charge me with a crime."

"I'm not going to charge you. Anyway, it would be Thea who would ask the police to press charges. But I'm very angry with you. Very angry."

What a fiasco. "Narin, I'm so, so sorry. I never meant—," I blubbered.

"Jane, relax. For heaven's sake. Thea's not going to charge you with any crimes. But still. This is quite serious.

"Listen carefully to me. You must figure out when and how you are going to confess to Thea what you've done on her behalf. I'm sure I don't need to tell you she'll be upset."

"I know. And I promise I'll tell her."

"I believe you want to. Tell me how and when you're going to do it."

"Should I call her now? As soon as I hang up with you?" My fingernails went straight into my mouth.

"I don't think that's the best approach. Don't ruin this retreat for her. To be frank, she might not even take your call."

If Narin had body-slammed me to the floor, I couldn't have felt more battered or breathless.

"Okay…What if I meet her flight at the airport and confess the minute she gets off the plane? Maybe in the meantime she'll avoid her phone and enjoy her vacation? Maybe she won't see any messages about what happened?"

"I suppose anything's possible," Narin said.

"Or, do you want to let her know? Since you're on good terms with her? You could break it gently—"

"Oh, no." She cut me off. "No way. This is entirely on you."

I didn't mean to get out of it. I just wanted Thea to be prepared. Narin was right; my instincts were horrible.

"Okay. I'll meet her at the airport and confess. If she's already discovered what I've done, well, I'll take what-ever she wants to throw at me when I meet her at baggage claim. I won't contact her until then, and I won't go back into her accounts, and I won't contact anyone about the jobs or anything. Whatever fallout she sees while she's on vacation, she'll be ready to lay into me when she gets back. In the meanwhile, I'll get ready to take it."

"That," Narin said, "is the wisest thing you've said all night."

As soon as I hung up, my face turned into Niagara Falls. I stumbled into the kitchen and located a party-sized bag of potato chips, which I took to bed with me.

My thoughts swirled. I wanted all the answers without having to ponder the questions. Licking the salt off my fingertips, I plunged my hand into the chip bag for more comfort.

Why wouldn't Thea tell me about her plans? Moreover, why would she tell Narin, who we hadn't known nearly as long, and specifically instruct her not to tell me? Every message, every idea that tried to display itself in my head seemed to be written in a foreign alphabet; I couldn't begin to comprehend anything.

I polished off the chips, then felt a bit sick. With tears still streaming and nose now running, I ran to the bathroom. A shower would make me feel better. I turned on the taps as hot as they would go and peeled off my clothes.

I stood under the showerhead and hoped the hot water spray would pound some sense into me. Steam rose all around me, loosening the tight muscles, making me sweat.

I braced my hands against the tile and tried not to think about anything but the spray.

Maybe she told Narin because Narin's an attorney? Maybe she was seeking legal advice on setting up the business? Possible. But it didn't explain why she ordered Narin not to tell me.

Lifting my face to the showerhead, the hot water rinsed the salt and crumbs off my lips and the salt tracks from my cheeks. The eco-warrior in my head warned I was wasting water; I told her to shut up. I needed to be on my own side for once.

Why, why, why were my instincts so wrong?

Why is it your job to save her? Narin had asked me the last time we spoke. Good question. I racked my brain, but I saw no clear answers. My gut told me maybe I should look elsewhere, but it might have been the potato chips talking.

My legs decided to check out for the night; they were tired of holding me up. I slid down the wall and sat in the bathtub, the shower now like fine needles pricking my neck, my shoulders, my outstretched limbs. I scooted to the opposite side of the tub, wedging myself between the tub faucet and the wall, and let the water trickle back over me as it searched for the drain.

I don't know how long I sat there. The one great thing about this hole I live in is that the hot water never ever runs out. I wallowed in the steam and the steady drumming, humming of the spray on the porcelain as it merged with the white noise in my head.

CHAPTER ELEVEN

I t was a surprise, to say the least, to wake up and find myself soaking wet in the shower. I shook my head, my wet hair stinging my cheeks like a towel snapped in a junior-high locker room. I uncurled myself—*ow, ow ow ow ow!*—, stretched, unfolded myself to standing, and shut off the water.

Fog dense as frozen yogurt hung in the bathroom. I yanked a towel off the rack and scoured my hair, then wrapped it around my head, turban-style. I grabbed another towel and scrubbed myself dry. When I opened the door, the chill of the air conditioner shocked goose pimples to my skin, and I sprinted for the bedroom to find something warm to wear.

The clock said 3:18. I wrapped myself in my heavy bathrobe, plunged back into my bed, and pulled the covers up to my neck.

The next time I woke up, the clock advised it was 10 a.m., a much more reasonable hour for a Saturday morning. I threw back the bedcovers—God, what had I been thinking?—and staggered to the kitchen to worship my Dark Lord: full-caff Colombian roast.

Thoughts of Thea and of Narin's words from last night buzzed around me like gnats. I poured a second bowl of Frosted Flakes and swatted the thoughts away. Not this morning. I was going to get out of the house, go someplace, do anything to get out of my head.

I felt weird taking a shower after I'd taken a shower most of last night, but going to bed damp, cold, and bundled up had left me sweaty and vile this morning. Thanking the universe for the small mercy that the water was included with the rent, I took another shower—short this time, to atone for last night's wastefulness—dressed in my favorite yoga pants and T-shirt, and walked right past my favorite yoga studio to catch the bus downtown.

I stopped in to feed Cleo, but she was hiding somewhere, and if I looked for her, I'd probably find trouble instead. So I filled her dish, sprinted out the door, and continued on my way.

Every year around the Fourth of July, when half of America's population decides it's time to pay tribute to our founders by feasting on funnel cakes and cramming themselves onto the DC subways, the Smithsonian holds its Folklife Festival on the Mall. While the timing is smart marketing on the Smithsonian's part, it's an equally good excuse for locals to continue to not enjoy their city's museums. Normally I don't do huge crowds, but I needed drastic measures to take my mind off everything I'd done.

The smells of grilled meat and bus fumes snuggled up to the tents and tucked themselves between buildings and bodies. As the sun beat down on me and what felt like millions of tourists, I tried to persuade myself that this had in fact been a genius idea.

I figured I could make the case more clearly to myself if I got out of the sun. So when I heard music drifting out of one of the tents, I went inside to investigate.

Several curved wooden xylophones waited on a dance floor. People sat behind them, all dressed in colorful tunics. Off to one side of the ensemble, a man began tapping on a large drum. The players seated behind the xylophones started to play.

The music sounded like bubbles drifting up from a deep spring. The notes rushed and tumbled, each clear and crisp, one after another. I sat down on the edge of the metal bleachers set up in the tent, closed my eyes, and let the melody wash over me. I imagined dipping my toes into a pool of cool water. Heavenly.

"Enjoying yourself?" someone asked in my ear.

I jumped a mile, startling the people around me. I turned to the source of the question.

It was the delivery guy.

I gasped, trying not to appear too obviously thrilled. "Hi. Um, yeah, the music's amazing, isn't it?"

"I love ranat," the guy said.

"Is that what it's called?" I asked.

"Shhh!" someone behind us said.

The delivery guy pretended to look sheepish and guilty, and he turned back to the performance. But not before he winked at me.

He winked. At me.

I couldn't pay attention to the music after that. I heard it, but I can't tell you what it sounded like, or even how many songs they played. I peeked at Delivery Guy out of the corner of my eye. His feet were propped on the bench in front of him, his elbows on his knees. His hands cupped his face. His dark hair fell across his forehead and into his eyes, but he didn't care. He was mesmerized.

So was I.

After the performance, he turned to me. "So, what did you think?"

"I thought it was amazing!" I said. "I loved the sound. It's so relaxing."

"The instruments they're playing? Normally, the bars are made out of rosewood or another hardwood. But the bars on these instruments are made out of bamboo, which of course is a grass. It produces a different sound."

"Huh," I said, looking back at the xylophones as if they might have some conversation tips for me. Instead of listening to them carefully, I blurted out the first idiotic observation that came to my mind. "I like the way they're shaped."

"Yeah, they're beautiful, aren't they? The curved shape is meant to suggest a riverboat."

"Oh! I can see that." I desperately needed solid conversational ground. "So, are you a musician?"

"Not really. It's just a hobby. I'm actually in grad school, studying anthropology."

"Wow." That's another subject I knew nothing about.

He smirked at me. "Next you're going to ask, 'So what do you plan to do with that,' right?"

"No, I wasn't," I lied.

"It's okay. Everyone asks. I'd like to work in a museum. Or maybe for *National Geographic*. I'd love to travel for my job."

"I love to travel."

"Yeah? Where have you been?"

"No place very interesting," I confessed. "But I'd like to."

"Where would you go if you could go anywhere?"

"Well, I've never been to Europe, so of course I want to go there. But I'd love to go on a safari in Africa. That's my secret dream."

"Secret dream, huh? That's mine, too. Only it's not so secret. I tell everyone, even people who don't ask. Sometimes especially people who don't ask."

His eyes drifted over me. I must have looked awful. My T-shirt came from a rock concert from years ago—the band wasn't even together anymore—and it was painted with pizza stains. My yoga pants mercifully covered my pale thighs, but not my calves, which were long overdue for a shave. I hugged my legs, hoping he hadn't noticed. Why had I thought it was acceptable to leave the house looking like this? My hair was wound in a sloppy bun, the short layers strapped down to my skull with bobby pins, because I hate when my hair gets sweaty and sticks to my face. It would have been quite useful at that moment to use my hair to hide my face, from which my makeup was sliding away like a luge on a training track.

We sat there, looking at each other. All the bodies packed into the tent made the humidity unbearable. Sweat stung my eyes.

"So, what's your name again?" he asked.

"Um." I couldn't believe it. For a moment, I totally forgot. You think such things only happen in movies, but I'm proof that being struck dumb is a very real disaster.

"You're not going to give me a fake name, are you?" he asked.

"No! No. My name's Jane." I pulled out my wallet. "See? Here's my driver's license to prove it."

"Not a bad picture, Jane," he said, examining the plastic card. "But you don't live near Jade Palace."

"What?"

"Jade Palace. The Chinese restaurant?"

"Oh! Of course. No, it's close to my friend's house. I was going there when I ran into you."

"Oh," he said.

"Her name's Thea," I said, in case he thought I went to see a guy. Smooth as a boulder-strewn highway, that's me.

"Do you live close to there?" I asked.

"On the same cross street. I go to American, so I live closer to the Wisconsin Avenue end. But it's convenient enough for a part-time job."

"Very convenient."

"Well, Jane Desmond of Connecticut Avenue, speaking of work, I have to get there. And I'd better go home and clean up before I do. But it was nice to run into you."

"Nice to run into you, too."

He brushed his hand through his hair and gave me a smile and a wave as he started off. His legs were tanned and nicely muscled; he must be a runner, I thought. It wasn't until he disappeared into the crowd that I realized I'd forgotten to ask his name.

I ducked into the National Gallery of Art to get out of the heat, which was making me dizzy. At least, I think it was the heat.

The gallery, of course, doesn't permit water bottles so I stood in line for the water fountain, trying to ignore the fat guy in front of me blanketing the sprayer with his slobbery lips. I let the water run for a few seconds before I lowered my mouth to drink.

I couldn't believe I didn't get Delivery Guy's name. He not only knew my name, my *whole* name, he also knew where I lived. Thea would have lectured me about being safe with my information, but of course, he would have known exactly where I lived if he delivered Chinese food to me. He's probably fine, I thought. Too cute to be a serial killer. Ted Bundy was an outlier.

I found a bench in the lobby and leaned back against the cool marble of the wall. Maybe later on, I would check on Cleo again. She was probably lonely. And maybe a little weirded out, with all the furniture gone.

Maybe I would stop by and pick up some takeout on the way home.

He was clearly interested, right? He wouldn't have come up to me out of nowhere if he wasn't interested. Although maybe he was just being polite. Either way, I couldn't stop by the restaurant without first going home to shower and change. Or would that make me too obviously interested? I couldn't win. My sloppy self—the part he'd just seen—well, who wanted that? If I hadn't been so gross, maybe he'd have stuck around longer. He said he had to get to work, but maybe that was just an excuse to flee the scene once he noticed my casual shaving habits? But if I went home to freshen up, I'd be trying too hard. And I'd have to make up a story about where I was going, all dressed up, and we've already established that lying is one of my primary fields of incompetence.

I spent the rest of the afternoon wandering between roasting festival exhibits and freezing museum lobbies. Around five o'clock, I started back home. I needed a shower before I visited Cleo. Because heaven forbid the cat found me sweaty and gross.

As I emerged from the Metro station, my phone rang: Mom's ringtone. I silenced it and sent it to voicemail; I didn't have the energy to fight off whatever social plans she'd made for me.

I dragged myself home and showered (for the third time today—thank God I'd never see that water bill!) before going to Thea's apartment. I put on a cute sundress and sandals, dried and curled my hair, and put on makeup. That cat better appreciate how good I looked.

On the bus to Thea's, I listened to Mom's voicemail.

"Hi, darling. It's your mother. Listen, Janet Wheeler and I are coming up there next weekend to see *Mama Mia*. Why don't you make a Saturday lunch reservation for the three of us someplace nice? Now that I think of it, make it four, and we can invite Paul Alexander along. His mother might have a bag of stuff to deliver to him, and as long as I'm coming up there, I might as well save her the UPS charges, right? I'll let you know for sure in a day or two. Oh, and speaking of stuff from home, bring your car to meet us because I've got three big Rubbermaid tubs of your stuff for you. I'm cleaning out the basement so your Dad and I have room to do tai chi. Love you. Bye-bye."

CHAPTER TWELVE

Naturally, when I passed by Jade Palace, Delivery Guy was nowhere to be seen. Cleo did not give two hoots about how nice I looked, so I fed her quickly, got out before I grew tempted to "help" Thea again, and went back home, where I put on my second-favorite set of yoga pants and second-favorite, but equally stained, T-shirt. Another hot night for a single woman in the city.

I spent the next week feeding Cleo, dodging Keith at work, and conveniently forgetting to involve Paul Alexander in my lunch plans with Mom. I anticipated the date much as one anticipates a root canal or a visit to the department of motor vehicles.

Saturday came, as it threatened it would. Dutiful as always, I drove down Connecticut Avenue in my Volkswagen Beetle to meet my mom and Mrs. Wheeler at their hotel. I had no idea how she hoped to cram three large boxes of my childhood memorabilia into my car, but Mom would find a way. Maybe she and Mrs. Wheeler could each hold one, and we could put one in the trunk.

Parking, of course, was valet or nothing. I pulled up next to the curb, put on my hazard lights, and waved the valet away. I called my mom. "I'm down here and there's nowhere to park. You'd better come down."

The valet knocked on my window. I rolled it down.

"I'm just waiting to pick up my mom. She's on her way down."

"You can't stay here," he said.

"I'll only be a minute," I said, rolling the window up. I couldn't waste energy fighting with the parking valet; surviving this lunch was going to take everything I had in me.

Mom and Mrs. Wheeler came out the front door, pushing a bellman's cart with, as promised, three plastic tubs piled on. Only they weren't the normal, laundry-basket-sized kind. She'd gotten the largest ones I'd ever seen, each big enough to hold a body. I got out of the car.

"Mom, I can't take those and you and Mrs. Wheeler. I can't even take one of those. You did remember I drive a bug, right?"

Mom pouted. "It's your stuff, Jane. I want it out of my house."

"Well, I can't put it in the car and take the two of you to lunch. Our reservation is in thirty minutes, and it's going to take at least half of that to park. You've got to take it back upstairs. We'll figure it out later."

Mrs. Wheeler shuffled her feet, her glance bouncing between mom and me. I felt a little sorry for her.

"Fine," Mom said, turning to push the cart. "I'll be down in a second."

"Do you need a hand?" Mrs. Wheeler asked.

"No, I've got it," Mom huffed. She shoved the cart toward the automatic doors, which parted to accept her and her haul in defeat.

"How are you, Mrs. Wheeler?" I asked, putting on a smile.

"I'm fine, dear."

"*Mama Mia*, is that right?"

"Oh, yes. Your mother and I listened to the soundtrack all the way up here."

"That must have been fun."

"Well, yes."

And there went that conversation topic, spent.

Mom reappeared, sprinting for the glass doors. She overshot the sensor and stopped short, waiting to be electronically recognized. The doors slid open and she squeezed through.

"Let's go," she said.

We buckled up, and I turned off the hazard lights. "Where are you taking us for lunch?" she asked.

"Georgia Brown's," I said. "They serve southern cuisine." Georgia Brown's is one of my favorite restaurants in DC. If I had to suffer through this lunch, at least I was going to enjoy my food.

"Southern food is fattening," Mom said.

"I'll bet they have a salad," Mrs. Wheeler said hopefully.

The ride was quiet. I let the restaurant valet park the car.

The hostess seated us at a table along the wall. "I'd hoped we could sit by a window," Mom said.

"We're not important enough for a window table, Mom," I joked.

"Look! Is that John McCain?" Mrs. Wheeler said, grabbing my wrist and pointing.

I looked. "No, ma'am. I think that's just another old guy."

"Oh," she said, disappointed.

"I'm sure we'll spot someone famous," I lied. "This is a big restaurant for the movers and shakers."

Mrs. Wheeler wiggled in her seat, like a kindergartener on a field trip. "Wouldn't that be exciting?"

I nodded and reached for my water glass. Maybe Mrs. Wheeler could be an ally here, a distracting influence.

"Hello, ladies." Our waiter bowed over our table, hands tucked behind his back. His blue eyes darted back and forth between us. "Welcome to Georgia Brown's. Is this your first time visiting with us?"

I shook my head. Mom and Mrs. Wheeler nodded vigorously, all smiles. He winked.

"Well—"

"What do you recommend today?" I wanted to keep things moving.

"What *don't* I recommend? We've got an heirloom tomato stack that is to die for, that comes with a local feta cheese and an organic maple-balsamic vinaigrette, plus a basil pesto and a bacon jam, for twelve dollars. There's also a seasonal oyster platter, served with a charred lemon aioli, a traditional pickle relish, and a corn bread beignet, for fifteen dollars. Can I start you off with something from the bar? Some Champagne, maybe a glass of chardonnay? Peach martini?" He batted his eyes at my mother, knowing a sucker when he saw one.

"Ooh, I'd love a glass of white zinfandel," Mom said.

"Would you like to see a list?"

"No, you pick one out," she said.

"I'd be delighted," he said. "And for you, ma'am?"

Mrs. Wheeler nodded. "White zinfandel sounds nice."

"Of course. And you, young lady?" he asked.

For God's sake. If we'd grown up together, I would have been his babysitter. But he was performing for my mom, and she was lapping it up like a cat after cream.

I glanced over the cocktail menu. "Bring me your Pauli's Island Iced Tea." It was their southern variation on a Long Island Iced Tea: just the fortification I would need.

"You don't want a glass of wine?" Mom said.

"I'm going to need something stronger," I murmured to the waiter.

He grinned at me. "Coming right up," he said and turned toward the bar.

"He's cute," my mother said at me. "I think he likes you. He called you 'young lady.'"

I rolled my eyes. "Mom, please. I'm older than he is, and he knows it. He wants a big tip."

"I think he's interested."

"He's not," I promised. "Mrs. Wheeler, what's new with you?"

She shook her head, lips pressed together and a slight shrug to her shoulders. "Nothing at all. You know Bishop's Creek. Not much going on."

"Of course," I said.

"Did you call Paul Alexander?" Mom asked.

"No, I did not."

"Patty said he's working for a law firm." She raised her eyebrows at me.

"So are half the people in this town," I pointed out.

"You might just call him."

"Mom, he's a grown man living his own life. Let's let him enjoy it."

"I don't know why you won't try, Jane."

"I try in my own way." Which was to say, not much, but at least I was independent. "Mrs. Wheeler, have you seen any good movies lately?"

She shook her head. "Nope. I think the last movie I saw in the theater was *Mrs. Doubtfire*."

"Oh, my," I said.

Our waiter came back with our drinks. "White zinfandel," he pronounced, setting two goblets full of pink liquid in front of the older women. "And a Pauli's Island Iced Tea."

"Thank God," I whispered.

"It's strong," he cautioned.

"It had better be," I said.

"Now, have we had time to consider the menu? Can I get anyone something to start off?"

"I'll have the tomato stack," I said. "And your devil shrimp and a side of succotash." I passed the menu back.

"Very good. And you?" he asked, turning to my mom.

"My lord, the prices," Mom said, her widening eyes magnified behind her reading glasses. She turned to Mrs. Wheeler. "I don't see a salad," she whispered, not so quietly. She's losing her hearing and what she thinks is quiet, isn't.

"You could have a vegetarian dish, Mom," I said.

"Well, what fun is that?" she asked.

"Maybe the chicken," Mrs. Wheeler said. "That's only twenty dollars. And chicken, you know. Unless it's got a cream sauce?" She scanned the menu again.

"You could have sea bass, then," I said. "Or salmon."

"They're both lovely," the waiter said.

"Oh, what the heck. I'll have the beef tenderloin," Mom said. "But could you do it without the chilies? And without the curry sauce? I bet it's hot. Is it hot curry?"

"Yes, it's spicy. It's very good, though," he said.

Mom shook her head. "I can't do heat. I still get hot flashes."

"We can certainly hold the spice," he said. "Would you like another side, then? Maybe the grilled asparagus?"

Mom hesitated, wanting to please the waiter. She's always hated asparagus. "Oh, sure. Why not?"

"Very good. The tenderloin is served medium rare. Is that okay?"

"Can you bring it well done?"

"Of course," he said.

After many inquiries and some deliberation, Mrs. Wheeler ordered the chicken. The waiter departed. I took a long, long sip of the iced tea. It couldn't hit my bloodstream fast enough.

Mom watched the waiter walk away. "He's so handsome. Maybe you could get his number."

I set my glass on the table, already half-empty. "I'm pretty sure he's gay."

"Oh, surely not," she said, her forehead wrinkling.

Mrs. Wheeler was making steady progress on her wine. "Lots of waiters are," she said helpfully. "Is that Newt Gingrich?"

"I think it might be," I said, reaching again for my glass.

Mom turned back to me. "Honey, why don't you try internet dating?"

"I'm sure I'll meet someone on my own, thanks."

"What does 'swipe right' mean?" Mrs. Wheeler asked me.

"I…" My head swiveled to her in an aural double take. "What?"

"Swipe right? Is that what you say?"

"Yes," I sighed, draining my glass. "It means you like someone. On dating apps, if you like someone's photo and profile, you swipe right to show your interest. If you don't, you swipe left."

"So you do know how it works," Mom confirmed.

"I would definitely swipe right on our waiter," Mrs. Wheeler giggled.

I checked my watch. We had been here twenty minutes. "Excuse me," I said. "I'd better go wash my hands."

"I'll join you," Mom said, scooting back her chair. "I need to—"

"How about this," I suggested. "Why don't I go first and figure out where the bathrooms are. Then when I get back to the table, you and Mrs. Wheeler can go. We don't want to appear as if we've abandoned our table, do we? Plus, I can tell you where they are so you don't have to ask the waiter."

"That's probably a good idea," Mrs. Wheeler said, finally coming to my rescue.

"Okay," Mom slurred, dragging her chair back up to the table.

I stood up. My feet already had started to tingle from the "iced tea," so I made a concerted effort to walk normally. I'm not great at holding my alcohol, and unfortunately, when I've had a few I find that tact slips out of my grasp like a greased pig. Also, my sophistication lapses.

The women's restroom was inviting, decorated like a posh living room with a few toilet cubicles tastefully obscured by heavy louvered doors. I sat in the lounge part, closed my eyes, and prayed for the end of the world.

Why, why, why couldn't I have a conversation with my mother that didn't involve my status in relation to a man? I'm a fully independent adult. I pay my bills, I hold my job, I stay out of jail. By any rational account, I am a successful human being. But Mom's only measure of success is whether I manage to get a ring on my finger and a fetus in my uterus.

Honestly, I don't think she's ever said to me, "I'm proud of your career." Okay, my gig at *Recycling World* may not be much in the grand scheme of things—not like, say, my former sorority sister Nina, who now works for the State Department in nuclear nonproliferation. But I've been promoted twice. I'm second in command of the flagship publication of Mercatur Media. Ask anyone in the construction-debris remediation industry. That's not nothing.

If this conversation were held with a casual friend, or

some cousin or aunt I saw only on major holidays, I wouldn't care. I could write it off. But you can't write off your mother. Or maybe *you* can, but I can't. No, I have to find a way to survive her.

From time to time I have a dream. In it, I'm dressed like Joan of Arc, riding fully armored on a white horse into battle. As I reach the crest of a grassy hillside, I spot my opponent in the valley below. The army is meager; I can count them on the fingers of one hand. My opponent rides a black horse and the lieutenant carries a massive silk banner, which flutters in the breeze. As the breeze stills, I see that the banner is embroidered with a pair of massive golden rings held in the mouths of a pair of doves. I draw my sword and raise it above my head. I'm ready to charge, but something holds me back. My opponent lifts the face guard on her helmet, and I see that it's Mom. She's plodding up the hill at a leisurely pace, as if she's leading a cow to a barn.

My arm falls to my side, fatigued from holding the sword aloft. It doesn't matter, because the sword's turned to jelly. Mom's horse ambles up to my side, and Mom gestures to the lieutenant. "Hi, sweetie," she says. "I got tired of waiting, so I found a nice man for you. I even picked out a house for you two to live in. It's right across the street from Dad and me so you won't have to carry your stuff very far." And she throws a lasso around my horse and me and pulls us along.

As we ride away, the other members of her army fall back to my side to guard me, the prisoner of war. One of them opens a binder with photos of wedding cakes. Mom pulls up short and turns in her saddle to look at me. "By the way, dear," she says, "that armor makes your waist look thick."

"Are you all right, madam?" a woman asked, touching my shoulder. I jolted.

"I'm fine," I lied. "I just needed a moment." My chin felt a bit moist; I wiped it with the back of my hand. Good Lord, had I been drooling?

"You were snoring," she said. She was dressed all in black, but her shirt had the restaurant's name and logo embroidered near her shoulder.

Of course I was. I looked around the lounge, but I was alone except for the restaurant employee. I couldn't have been here long; Mom and Mrs. Wheeler would have found me first. I shook my head and stood up.

"Whoof," I said. "That's the last time I work until two a.m. on a Friday night!" I smoothed my blouse down and checked myself over her shoulder in a floor-to-ceiling mirror. "I'd better get back to the table. My lunch is probably served!" I bolted before she could say anything else.

Walking back through the now-crowded restaurant, dodging tourists with large day packs and waiters with heavily laden trays, proved to be more difficult than I'd expected. Not only were they now slightly unfocused, but so was I. I had only a tenuous grasp on where my sides ended and open space began. Across the room, I made out my mother, standing anxiously at our table, shielding her eyes from imaginary glare as she searched for me.

"There you are!" she shouted as I approached the table. "I was starting to think you'd fallen in."

"Nope!" I said, misjudging the drop to my chair.

"Are you okay?"

"Just a little tired. I was up late last night. Working," I said, anticipating her next question.

"You work all the time," she pointed out.

"I do," I said.

"You must really love your job," Mrs. Wheeler said.

"It's—" I had to stop myself from reflexively telling the truth. My purported love of job was the only thing shielding me from more strategizing about how to resolve my lackluster love life. "It's something, to be second-in-command at a major industry publication." There! Not a lie, not entirely true. Exactly where I like to live.

"Don't pull at your necklace, dear, you'll strain the clasp," Mom said. She finished her white zinfandel and looked around the room for the waiter.

"Hey, so, if you want to go to the ladies' room, it's around that corner, the third door on the right," I said. "It's really nice in there."

"Let's go," Mrs. Wheeler said. "I'm going to pop soon."

The older ladies left the table, giving me a moment to try to collect myself. What else could we talk about? Mom would love to know about Thea, of course, but that topic might invite her to critique my interventions on Thea's behalf thus far. The weather, obviously, was an option. Her tai chi ambitions? No, that would bring us back to the bins of my unwanted junk. Didn't she say she was playing tennis again? Or we could try to talk about *Mama Mia*. I didn't remember any Abba songs besides "Dancing Queen." Would Mom and Mrs. Wheeler, empowered by white zin, attempt to refresh my melodic memory? All we had to do was make it until the food was served. Then we could talk about lunch.

Mom and Mrs. Wheeler returned at the same time as our waiter, who toted a tall, collapsible luggage stand. Another waiter trailed behind him, carrying the food. Our waiter opened the stand to relieve the lesser waiter of his burden, then pulled out my mother's chair for her.

"Oh, good!" my mother squealed as our waiter scooted her up to the table. He did the same for Mrs. Wheeler. I kept my eyes on the food.

"Tenderloin, well done," he said, setting Mom's plate before her. "And the chicken," he bestowed on Mrs. Wheeler.

"Looks good," I said.

"And the tomato stack and succotash." He straightened up, and the lesser waiter whisked away the tray and stand. "Anything else I can offer you at this time? Would you like another white zinfandel?"

"I would," Mom said.

Mrs. Wheeler nodded.

"Another Pauli's Island Iced Tea?" he asked me, his mouth curling at one side.

Could I ride this buzz once I started eating the food? Would it sustain me? God, they'd want dessert, too. The place was packed, and service would surely slow down. I made a strategic assessment. "Can I have a half one?"

"I'm sure we can do that for you," he said, winking and turning on his heel.

The tomato stack was gorgeous, but looking across the table at my dining companions, I recognized a deep need for animal protein. Hadn't I ordered some? I couldn't remember. I hoped Mom would offer me a bite. She usually likes to trade bites.

Our group, mercifully silent, dug in. Mrs. Wheeler cut her entire chicken into tiny, equal-sized bites and arrayed them neatly on the plate before she began. Mom sawed heartily at her tenderloin and ignored the pile of asparagus at her elbow.

"It must be good," I said, swallowing a mouthful of tomato. "Everyone's quiet."

Mrs. Wheeler nodded happily, putting one dainty bite of chicken into her mouth.

Our waiter came back with our drinks. "How is everything?"

We nodded, mouths full. The tomato stack was genuinely delicious, so I gave him a thumbs-up.

"And here's your half-sized iced tea," he said, setting it next to me. A busboy filled our glasses from a sweaty silver pitcher wrapped in a heavy linen napkin. I barely saw him.

"Take it easy," he said in a cheerful way, patting my shoulder.

"You too!" I called after him, my mouth still full of tomato.

Mrs. Wheeler drank from her wine glass as she watched the waiter depart. "Jane, have you tried being gay? Maybe that would work."

I swallowed, and my temples throbbed. It was noisy in here. "What did you say?"

"I said," she hollered, "have you tried? Being? Gay?"

I wiped my mouth and blinked at her. Where to start? This was a greater job than I was capable of handling, at least today. "No, ma'am," I said.

Mom shook her head. "No no no. She needs to settle

down. She has to get married so I can have grandchildren."

Here, you see, were her priorities laid bare. My emotional well-being was not a concern here. Mom needed an excuse to buy cutesy baby clothes like all her friends did. I gulped my refreshed iced tea for courage and got ready to set them straight. There was so much to cover.

"First, my being gay would not make the waiter like me. That's not how it works. Second, gay people can get married, *and* they can have kids. Third—" I was losing track of the illogical conclusions she'd drawn. "Right. Third, you don't have to be married to have children and be a good parent. There are loads of good single parents out there. Fourth, I don't even know if—"

Mom shook her head. "Nope. I don't want adopted kids. I want blood relatives."

"You can have a donor."

"Is that what you want? A kid with a stranger? Who knows who that person could be. He could be a serial killer."

"Mom, for God's sake—"

"And anyway, you'll need two donors if you keep waiting. You don't have much time left. Your eggs are getting old."

"Why are we having this conversation?" I shouted. "Can't we talk about anything else?"

Mom and Mrs. Wheeler looked at each other.

"Like what?" Mom asked.

I was out of ideas. I was also out of energy, of defense, of internal physical structure. My bones had melted. If the waiter came by and put his thumb on my head, he could have smeared me into the table and out of existence, like a gnat. A quick flick of his linen towel and I'd be gone without a trace. A mercy killing. Then he could sit down and explain modern relationships to Mom and Mrs. Wheeler.

I laid my head on the table. With my right hand, I waved my napkin in the air.

"Is that a signal for the check?" The waiter appeared miraculously at my side.

"Yes, please," I begged him.

"No dessert?"

Mrs. Wheeler looked across the table and me and patted my hand. "Maybe we can get a slice of cake to go."

I threw my credit card at the waiter—I didn't even look at the check, I just wanted everything to be over—and stood up. It would have been more successful had I still had feet, but they'd been stolen. Mom and Mrs. Wheeler didn't seem to notice. They gathered their purses and their reading glasses and their cake and levered themselves out of their chairs. I followed behind, gripping the backs of each chair I passed like a mountain climber grips the crevices in the rock face on the way to the summit.

As we approached the door, the waiter appeared next to me. "Here's your card," he whispered, tugging my elbow. "And you need to sign?"

He held the black notebook open for me while I scrawled something. Calculating a tip was unthinkable. "Give yourself something nice," I said, and patted him on the wrist as I stumbled after my mother.

On the sidewalk, Mom approached the valet. "Where's your ticket?" she asked me.

I shook my head. "We'll take a cab."

"But your car—"

"I'll come back and get it later."

We rode in silence back to the hotel. Once there, I followed them upstairs to Mom's room, locked myself in the bathroom, turned on the fan, ran the water in the sink, threw up my entire lunch, flushed it away, washed my hands and face, borrowed Mom's toothbrush to brush my teeth (I cleaned it with soap first), used up all her hotel mouthwash, collected my tubs of clutter she'd brought me, and took them in a cab back to my apartment.

"Have fun at the show," I said as I ducked into the backseat of the cab.

"Don't forget to get your car," Mom replied.

CHAPTER THIRTEEN

I woke up that evening, of course, with a blinding headache and a mouth full of cotton balls. I took four ibuprofens, downed a glass of water, and went back to sleep.

Sunday morning I got up early, having kept nothing in my stomach since yesterday's breakfast, and feasted on leftover pizza and applesauce. The three tubs from mom's basement sat just inside the door. Did the cabbie help me get them upstairs? I guess there are decent people left in the world. I hope I tipped him well.

My reflection in the toaster didn't look like a person I would aspire to be. In the bathroom mirror, I didn't look much better—still bulbous and bloated, only slightly less distorted.

Once again, I needed to get out of the house. I cleaned myself up, put on an old, loose-fitting printed top and some shorts, and went downstairs. I dropped by Thea's apartment to feed Cleo, then found myself wandering around bookstores in Dupont Circle.

I like browsing in bookstores. My favorite hobby, in fact, is to buy books and add them to the stack on my nightstand to collect dust. One day, I tell myself, I'll read them all. I'll cash in my accrued vacation, fill my car with all my unread books, drive out to Rehoboth Beach, and read until I turn the last page of the very last book.

I picked up *Pride and Prejudice*, which I already owned in paperback, but this one had a beautiful cover that made me weak in the knees. I contemplated purchasing a book on how to paint in watercolors, since that's another unfulfilled ambition of mine, but I set it down to go to the ladies' room, and when I came back someone had nicked my copy.

I turned a corner into a new section and stared at the shelves.

"Can I help you find something?" a clerk asked.

"No," I snapped. Guilt instantly attacked me; the clerk was only doing his job. "Sorry. I'm just browsing." I'd wandered into the self-help section, the worst place to be caught browsing.

"Of course. Enjoy," he said, disappearing behind a tall wooden shelf.

So, the self-help section may be the worst place to be caught by anyone you know, or anyone you don't know, for that matter, but between you and me, they had a lot of intriguing stuff.

One book promised three weeks to self-esteem, but I didn't need that kind of help. I liked me pretty well as is; unfortunately, everyone else saw opportunities in me for reform. Was there a book called *Getting Everyone On Your Page*?

Another book promised to declutter my mind. I was getting warmer, but let's be honest: I'd probably misplace it. What I really needed was someone to declutter my apartment. When I found one called *Difficult Conversations: Talking about Life's Most Important Things,* I thought I was on to something. But neither the table of contents nor the index mentioned anything about How to Politely Tell Your Mother to Stop Fixing You Up. Nor was there an entry for Office Creeps. And it was five hundred pages long. Back on the shelf it went.

Coping with Your Difficult Older Parent wasn't quite right. Mom didn't have dementia; she was just pushy. *Successful Interpersonal Dynamics* might have had useful advice, but when I opened it up, the pages were set in two columns per page, in tiny type. Sorry.

Emotional Vampires: Dealing with People Who Drain You Dry. Now this was more like it. But when I picked up what I thought was the last copy, I saw that I'd grabbed a book-shaped box sat there as a placeholder. A card attached to the front promised that more had been ordered. I'd have to come back.

There were endless titles for burned-out moms, for people fearful of public speaking, and for women who hated their bodies, were recovering from emotional abuse, or were getting over breakups. Lots of books had the words "Diva" and "Goddess" in the title, but, come on, I didn't want to find my inner queen. I laughed when I saw *Women Who Think Too Much.* Was that the book for me? Or maybe my problem was the opposite. Maybe I needed *Women Who Don't Think Enough.*

I started to spiral down a mental black hole on that question, so I decided to ditch the bookstore and head for brunch.

A corner bistro filled with dark wood paneling and strong air conditioning offered a promising place to hide. I tucked into a corner table, grasped the cup of coffee almost before the waitress finished pouring it, and cracked open *Pride and Prejudice.* My old friends the Bennett sisters knew a thing or two about people wanting to set you up.

But as I dipped into Austen's prose, for the first time I could remember, I couldn't get comfortable. Lines that reliably used to tickle my ribs felt more like punches to my gut. I know times were different back then; women of their social class didn't get jobs or have other means of personal fulfillment. Getting married was their job. But the story wasn't amusing anymore, and even Elizabeth's feistiness failed to cheer me. I mopped up my eggs with the crust of my toast and signaled to the waitress for more coffee.

A woman, younger than me by perhaps five years, approached the table. "Hi. Sorry to ask, but are you alone?" She wrinkled her nose at *alone* as if it smelled unwashed.

"I am," I said.

"Okay if I take your extra chair, then?" she asked, wrapping her hands around its back and lifting it up before I could agree. "Since you're not using it."

"No," I said, surprising myself.

"What?" she asked, bending closer and putting a hand to her ear. Nice touch.

I spoke up, since the poor thing's hearing was obviously impaired. "I said, NO."

She looked around as though to summon backup, then, seeing none, she coughed. That not-a-real-cough kind. "You're not using it. Are you expecting anyone? Is someone coming late?"

"No," I said.

"Then why—"

"Put my chair down," I said, rising to my feet and enunciating carefully. I donned my darkest crazy-lady face, the one I usually reserve for use on public transportation.

She curled her lip at me. "Bitch." She dropped my chair, straightening her fingers as if the wood had singed her flesh. She stomped off to her table. The four women seated there turned in unison to scowl at me, tossing their flat-ironed hair and squinting their lined eyes. I blew them a kiss.

"Can I get you anything else?" the waitress asked me, filling my water glass.

"Yes," I said, considering the women in their skinny jeans. "I'd like a cinnamon roll, please."

I put my feet up on my other chair and ate the pastry slowly, savoring every raisin and every flake of sugar. I picked it apart, rationing the bites until the table of women finished and paid their check. Then I asked the waitress for my bill, paid it, and left. I gave her a generous tip.

Back out on the sidewalk, the fresh air and bright sun hit me like a bus. But the impact didn't last long. As I wandered back to the Metro station, the clouds gathered in my head again.

At home, I polished off a carton of ice cream from the freezer and did some laundry. Focusing on big ideas was beyond my capacity right then, so I thought about more pressing concerns instead: Thea would be coming home in a few days, and that would be yet another mess to clean up. I'd pick her up at the airport and confess everything. I wouldn't even ask her questions about her new job.

What could the job be, though? She had good ideas. Maybe once she got it off the ground, she'd let me come work with her. We could be partners. But I wouldn't bring it up. Not at the airport, anyway.

CHAPTER FOURTEEN

I could tell when I saw Thea coming down the escalator at baggage claim that the vacation was, contrary to my belief, exactly what she needed. I hadn't added to my sins by snooping for her flight itinerary: she'd left her travel details on her kitchen counter, next to the instructions for feeding Cleo. So I drove out to Dulles to meet her, hoping she'd be happy to see me.

She looked relaxed, hopeful, even serene. She radiated so much positive energy, if you hooked her up to a generator she could have powered our tiny hometown, a one-woman clean-energy solution. That thought made it even harder for me to tell her what I'd done; I'd turn the situation from a sunny day to nuclear winter in a snap.

"Jane!" Thea exclaimed as she saw me walking toward her. "You came to meet me. I've really missed you." She wrapped her arms around me and gave me a big hug. "You know, I'm not sure we've ever been out of contact for two whole weeks."

"I don't think we have," I said, plastering on a big grin. "I missed you, too. It felt like I'd lost an appendage."

"You didn't have to come all the way out here."

"I wanted to." It wasn't entirely untrue: I wanted to see her. I didn't want to see what she was going to do to *me* when I confessed.

We dragged her suitcase off the conveyer belt, and I wheeled it to the car for her, while she lugged her monstrous carry-on bag.

"You look amazing," I said. "So relaxed. Tell me about your trip."

"It was fantastic. Just what I needed. I spent the first two days sleeping late, eating, and sitting on the beach. The water is unbelievably blue—bluer than those travel magazine photos can convey. You have to see it in person."

"Wow."

"They had free fitness classes so I took some yoga. I can't believe I never took a yoga class before. And I started meditating. I got an app, and I spent two entire days at it. Okay, more like twenty minutes at a time, but several times a day. I was hooked! It was hard at first, but by the end of the vacation I had the hang of it. And it's easier to do in a place where you have no distractions. I sat on the balcony of my hotel room and listened to the waves and breathed. I'm telling you, I feel like a new person. You should try it."

"Yeah, I've been meaning to," I said, adding yoga and meditation to my mental self-improvement list. I pulled out onto the road.

"I feel so much more peaceful now," she went on. "After I lost my job, I was in turmoil. You saw me, I couldn't do anything. I obsessed about it all day long, but I couldn't bring myself to act."

"I noticed that." Maybe this wasn't going to be as bad as I thought.

"I know. And you were really nice, trying to buck me up. I wasn't very patient with you when you were trying to motivate me. I'm sorry."

"It's fine. Don't give it a second thought. I'm just glad to see the old you coming through." The winch that had cranked my shoulders together for weeks unwound a tick or two.

"So, yeah. I feel like this is the old me, but better," she said. "The time and space gave me an opportunity to reflect. The downsizing shocked me, but it's nothing more than a bad surprise. My day-to-day happiness doesn't depend on that job. I don't have to tell you, I'm sure, that I'll never be passionate about processing insurance claims. Nope, this vacation's got me fired up. I'm ready to go out and seize happiness by the throat and say, 'You're coming with me, baby.'" She clapped her hands.

Old Thea was back! Only it was more like Thea 2.0, debugged, improved, and more powerful than ever. And headed in a totally new direction.

"Wow," I said.

"You know it."

"So...it sounds like you're ready for something new?" We pulled to a stop at a light, and I glanced at her.

"Yes!"

"That's exciting." I drummed my fingers on the steering wheel. How was I going to approach this? "Tell me about it?"

The light turned green.

"I will," she said. "But first, I need to check my email. I was so good while I was on vacation. They had wi-fi, of course, but I took a digital sabbatical to relax and think. It was transformational. I think I'm going to practice a digital sabbatical every week now."

Yikes! I had to act fast, before she logged in and found anything. I took a deep breath. Do it. Just get it over with. The speech I'd practiced in my head on the way to the airport spluttered out of my mouth.

"Thea? Remember how you said that I was trying to motivate you, and how you appreciated it?"

"Yeah…" She dug in her bag for her phone.

"And how you said you wanted something new?"

"Uh-huh. Here it is!" She pulled her phone from the bag and held it in front of her. "It looks strange to me now. I wonder if I remember my passcode?"

"And, you know, we've known each other a long time. We can tell what the other one is thinking? Most of the time?"

"Yeah. Let's see." She punched in a series of numbers. "Shoot!" She turned to me. "I actually don't remember my passcode. Isn't that remarkable? I have to think about this. I don't want to lock myself out." She sat back and closed her eyes but instantly turned back to me, her eyes popping open. "Unless you remember it?"

It was 1999, because she loved Prince, but I'd eat my own gallstones before I told her.

"It'll come to you eventually. Just wait," I said. "So, while you were gone, I worried about you—"

"Oh, Jane. I know you did," she said, resting her hand

on my arm. "You're really kind to be so concerned. Ooh! I remember it." She punched in some numbers, humming the song's tune as her home screen popped up. "My goodness. Look at all the notifications."

"And I thought about how great your house was, and how paralyzed you were when you left. My anxiety got the better of me. I...I couldn't think straight." My voice broke, and a tear rolled out of my eye. She was going to kill me. She'd probably beat me senseless with her half-ton carry-on.

"Sweetie. Are you crying?" She glanced over at me to pat me on the arm, but her eyes darted back to her phone screen. Her hand fell back into her lap. "I'm going to be fine. Really. I know I acted weird for a while, but I just needed time away. The whole downsizing threw me for a loop, but I'm clear-headed now. I'm a new person. Don't worry."

"I couldn't help it," I said. "It's my nature to worry."

"True." She reached over again to squeeze my hand on the steering wheel.

"So, out of concern, I did something for you. I shouldn't have done it, but like I said, I couldn't think straight. I tried to get the ball rolling for you while you were gone."

"Get the ball rolling? What do you mean?" she said, looking up from her phone.

I had to do it now, just like I told Narin.

"When I was feeding Cleo, I followed her into your room, and I saw your resume that someone had marked up. I didn't paw through your stuff. It was just there. And I took it home, and I typed up the changes and posted it to your LinkedIn and your Facebook accounts. Because I promised to help with networking. I thought it would be good to let other people know you were looking, while you were upset. I meant well, and the changes were good ones, so I did it for you. I'm sorry."

"You updated my resume and posted it on my social media without asking me?"

"Yes," I said in the tiniest voice. "I shouldn't have done it. I'm so, so sorry." I was really crying now.

Her phone lay in her lap as she looked out the window.

When Thea gets angry, she gets really quiet, and then explodes. It's like an inferno that sucks all the oxygen up before it shatters the doors and windows, hurling splinters of wood and glass everywhere.

"Are you furious at me?" I asked.

"That was really out of line." Her voice was almost a whisper.

"I know. It was presumptuous and arrogant of me."

"Yes, it was." There was an edge to her voice.

She didn't say anything for at least a mile. We passed new apartment complexes under construction, where the pounding of jackhammers mirrored my nerves.

As we approached our exit, she spoke again. "I guess… I guess it's okay. I'd rather have told people in my own way."

"I didn't think of that. I'm sorry."

"Look, forget it. As long as you just posted the changes I was going to make anyway, I suppose there's no real harm in that. It's early days. I'll be overhauling it soon."

Was that it? Had her meditation practice transformed her temper? Could I possibly have dodged a missile here?

"I thought so!" I said, exhaling a huge breath. "I thought, 'I'll do this one thing, but she'll take it and run with it.' HR takes forever, you know, and I thought I could help by putting your news on people's radar screens."

The fist gripping my stomach loosened its hold, but only a little. I wasn't done; I couldn't be off the hook just yet.

She picked up her phone and scrolled through her notifications. "There's a lot of stuff from LinkedIn, actually."

"Oh?" I said. "So, maybe it's a good thing, like—"

"Wait. 'Your application has been received.' What does that mean? What application?" She clicked on the message and the app opened.

"Maybe it sent your resume to something automatically?" The invisible fist started kneading my stomach again. "I don't know how apps work."

"Huh. It appears that someone has applied for a managerial position at Kaiser for me." She turned toward me. I focused deeply on the car in front of us. Was that smoke I smelled? I hoped it was coming from the old Dodge minivan in front of us, and not, say, from my flesh being burnt by the stare aimed in my direction.

"You wouldn't know anything about that, would you?" she murmured.

I furrowed my brow like I was thinking hard, but who was I kidding? I needed to come clean. It was going to hurt, like that time I botched the home-waxing job on my lip and left a clump of hard wax in the cleft below my nose. You know it's going to sting like hell, but you have to finish it, because you can't go to work with a smudge of wax under your nose like a blue Hitler 'stache.

I took a deep breath and let it out. My heart raced.

"Jane?"

"I was getting to that. So what happened was, I posted the resume and almost immediately someone responded that there was a position opening up at Kaiser, and she thought you'd be perfect for it. So I asked for the job description—"

"You what?!"

"JUST so you would have it to consider when you came home. I wasn't going to prepare a cover letter or anything. I mean, I barely understand what it is you do. But she sent back a link to the actual application, asking for your contact information and your resume. There was a place for a cover letter, but I didn't touch that at all. That's totally not my place."

"*None* of it is your—"

"And like we just agreed, HR departments take forever, right? I thought, Thea will be back in two weeks. I'll have the description for her, she can reach out to the hiring person, and it'll be fine. In the meantime HR wouldn't even *look* at the application. So I filled in your name and contact information and attached the resume. Then I had second thoughts. No, I shouldn't do any of this. This is none of my business."

"You were right there," she said.

"I got up to fix myself some lunch, and when I got back to the table, I knocked over some mail on my table, and it took the mouse with it. When I grabbed the mouse I accidentally submitted the application, but without a cover letter. But look, by the time HR finds it, *if* they find it at all, you'll have your letter in the right people's hands. I mean, let's be honest, if the hiring people noticed a letter was missing they'd blame it on HR, not you. So it doesn't even matter, right? I shouldn't have done it, I know I shouldn't have done it, but the submission part was an accident. I was going to remove it, honestly. I'm really sorry. I'm sorry I'm sorry I'm sorry I'm sorry I'm sorry."

I heard the back draft sucking in through her nostrils.

"JANE DESMOND! How could you?!" she screamed. "You had no business doing that! That was the nosiest, most presumptuous—"

"I know." I had to pull over; I couldn't see the road. I put my signal on to turn into a parking lot.

"Most busybody—aaarrgh! I can't *believe* you!"

"I wish I could take it back."

"But you can't! You always do stuff like this!"

I pulled into a parking spot and put the car in park. "What? No, I don't."

"You always take things too far. Most of the time it's just annoying. It's like when we were kids, and you brought home every damned bird that had fallen out of its nest. I'm not a helpless baby bird, okay?"

"But I was—"

Thea leaned over and stabbed her finger in my shoulder.

"Why do you think you have to take stuff into your own hands? You're not my mom. I'm a grown woman. I'm thirty-five years old. I can manage my own life."

"I know."

"You, on the other hand, can't manage your own life! Why do you feel like you can manage mine? You have no sense of goddamned boundaries! Do you even realize that?"

I opened my mouth to argue, but—mercifully—nothing came out.

"I suppose it's my fault," she said, sitting up straighter, lifting her chin. "I let you pull things, like cutting the tags out of my shirts when we come home from shopping."

"I did that once! You were complaining all the way home from the mall about how those tags itched."

"Or texting Richard after he and I argued, telling him to go easy on me because I had a hard week at work."

"But you had!"

"This isn't seventh grade! I don't need you to talk to my boyfriend on my behalf. What the hell? You didn't even like him."

"But I—"

"Or when we were at the party at Narin's house on Memorial Day? You tried to talk me out of buying my townhouse. You wanted me to buy the condo in Dupont Circle. You called the real-estate agent and asked her to give me an extra day to think it over. I knew what I wanted!"

"You said you were feeling jittery about the decision. What's the harm in asking for an extra day to be certain?"

"It's the principle of the thing. You think you're being thoughtful, supportive, taking little actions on my behalf, but really, you're just invading my space. How dare you second-guess me like that? It's my fault," she said, raising her hand, accepting blame. "I should have put a stop to this before now."

My mouth hung open. "I had no idea—"

"Do you think I would take off on a two-week vacation if I couldn't afford it? Do you think, after knowing me practically my whole life, that I would risk something I worked so hard to achieve?"

"Well, it didn't seem—"

"Did you ever pause to consider whether I might not want to work in insurance for the rest of my life? That I might have a Plan B? Did you ever imagine that I might have enough money stashed away to cover myself for a while?"

"But I asked, and you yelled at me. I didn't want to ask about money again. Because that would be—"

"Too intrusive? Remarkable. You recognize that asking personal questions is out of bounds, yet you can rationalize applying for a job on my behalf?" She slammed her back into the seat of the car and turned to stare out the window.

"It was an accident."

"No, it wasn't." She banged her hand on the glove compartment. "You believed you had the right to do it. I let little things slide, even not-so-little things, like Richard, or the real-estate agent. And every time you go a little further, it gives you permission to intrude more deeply into my life. If I let you off the hook for this, next week you'll be applying for things for me left and right."

"No, I wouldn't. If I saw that you were doing things on your own—"

"Let's be honest, shall we? Let's acknowledge that you can't keep your hands off my life because it's safer than tampering with your own. Why should you assume the risk? You think I don't know you're unhappy at goddamn

Recycling World? That's not exactly your dream job, is it? You're taking risks with my career because you're too scared to take them with yours."

"That's not true! I was afraid of seeing you suffer—"

"Suffer? I'll tell you how I'd be suffering. If I were stuck in a soul-killing insurance job the rest of my life. Yeah, it's predictable, it's safe. I can make decent money. But you know what? If I got hit by a bus tomorrow, I'd consider myself a failure. I'm tired of waiting for life to happen to me. I'm going to make a real change."

"What kind of change?" Maybe the worst was over. And I'd been dying to know, ever since Narin slipped up and told me. Thea always had fascinating ideas. Maybe—

She laughed, a short, angry bark. "You think I'm going to tell you about my new plans? So you can, what? Take over, launch the whole damned thing for me without asking for my input? No thanks."

I wiped my face with my sleeve because, of course, I'd forgotten to put tissues in my car. As I sat there, I realized she was right. She had a great idea, clearly something she felt passionate about. I'd asked about it, partly from curiosity, sure, but even in the midst of this blistering, my mind had gone there: Maybe I could help.

This was why she'd told Narin not to tell me.

"I'll take you home," I said. "Cleo will be happy to see you."

We didn't say another word the whole ride back from Dulles. I pulled up to her apartment building and put the car in park. "Home again," I said.

"Yes. But not for long."

"When do you have to be out?"

"End of the month," she said, opening the door and kicking her legs out.

"Do you want me to help you with your bags?"

"No, I've got it," she said, slamming the door. "Just pop the trunk." Through the window glass, she sounded far away.

I obeyed. I watched in the mirror as the trunk lid dragged upward on its hydraulic hinges, hissing all the way. She wrestled the enormous suitcase out of the back of the car and dropped it onto the pavement. She slammed the lid and looped the straps of her carry-on over the retracting suitcase handle. She leaned into it, shifting the load into motion.

She opened the passenger door again and stuck her head in. But she didn't look me in the eye.

"Do me a favor," she said. "Don't call me for a while. Don't text me. Don't do anything. I'll call you, if and when I'm ready." She kept her eyes on the gearshift.

I nodded. "Thea, I really am sorry. I can't tell you how much."

She jerked her chin in acknowledgment. "Good-bye," she said and shut the door.

CHAPTER FIFTEEN

s I looked in my mirror to pull away from the curb, I heard a knock on my passenger window. It was Thea again. I rolled the window down.

"Yes?" How was she going to kick me this time? I was so low by now, I was two-dimensional.

"Actually, Jane, could you wait here for a minute? There's something upstairs I want you to have."

"Sure," I said. And she turned up the sidewalk and yanked her bags inside.

I couldn't imagine what was left in the apartment she wanted me to have. A Diet Coke and a trash bag full of used kitty litter?

I sat there, staring at the Phish and Grateful Dead stickers on the beat-up Toyota Camry parked in front of me. The owner walked up, keys in hand, and unlocked the door. Out of the corner of my eye, I noticed him turn and walk toward my car. Instinctively, I locked the door, hoping that the sound of the electric locks wasn't so loud as to give offense.

"Jane?" he said. I turned, remembering the voice but praying it was an alien imposter coming to Earth to drag me away. But that would be inconsistent with my brand of luck.

Delivery Guy took a step closer to my car and ducked down to look in my open window. So much for locked doors.

"Yeah. Hi. It's me." I ran a hand through my hair. It was tangled and matted from driving back from Dulles with the window open. Between my Medusa-like hair and my splotchy, makeup-free face, I'm sure I looked irresistible.

"How're you doing?" he asked, squatting down to talk to me face-to-face. "I haven't seen you since the festival." He looked around. "Are you waiting on something?"

"My friend, Thea. I just brought her home from the airport, and she told me to wait because she has something for me. I don't know what it could be. She's moving out in a few days, and there's almost nothing left in her apartment."

Delivery Guy bit his lip. "Maybe she got you a present wherever she went?"

"Doubt it."

I didn't want him to see me looking like something freshly dredged from the bottom of the Potomac, but I did want to see his adorable face. I tried to strike a balance, peeking at him without turning my head. As it occurred to me that I must look like a sulky toddler checking to see if anyone was paying attention to her tantrum, he said, "Are you okay? Is something wrong with your neck?"

I think it was Winston Churchill who once advised, "When you're going through hell, keep going."

"You caught me at a bad time," I confessed, glancing up at him. "My friend and I just had a terrible argument."

"Oh. Well, I wouldn't know anything about that. I've never argued with a friend before."

He smiled at me, an actual sympathetic smile. That, plus the fact that he hadn't sprinted away at the sight of me, gave me a burst of courage. "So, you know, I keep running into you and you know my name, but I don't know yours. I only know you as the Chinese Delivery Guy."

"I'm not Chinese."

"No, I know you're not Chinese," I said, flustered. "I mean—" and then I realized he was kidding me. Would I never learn to pick up on these things in the moment?

He laughed at me, which, to be fair, I deserved. I made a face at him, which made him laugh harder.

"Okay," he said, sobering up. "Fair enough. My name's Howard."

"Howard," I said, trying to mask the combination of shock and disgust that must have been clearly written on my disastrous face. He was too cute to be a Howard. I couldn't be in bed with him screaming, "Oh, Howard! Howard! Yes!" It wouldn't work. I'd have to give him a nickname.

I tried to put on a face that said I'm cool with that, I don't care. People are naming their kids things like Maude nowadays. His parents were thirty years ahead of the curve.

"You don't hear that name so often anymore," I observed. "It's cool. In an old-fashioned way. Retro." I could have said worse.

His mouth curled at one side.

"What now?" I asked.

He started laughing again. He had a really cute laugh, especially for someone called Howard, who I thought should have more of a bray. "Just kidding," he said. "Howard's my last name."

"So what's your—" I started, but Mr. Howard wasn't looking at me anymore. As I turned to see what captured his attention, my passenger door flew open and a blizzard of paper blew in at me.

"There!" Thea screamed as stuff tumbled everywhere. "Take your bossy, controlling, none-of-your-fucking-business notes and charts and diagrams and shove them up your ultra-tight ass! *Fuck you!*"

You know how in movies or TV ads, when time suddenly goes into super slow motion and the glass of wine that's going to get spilled over the head of the woman wearing the snowy evening gown goes gliding through the air? And as it tips, the red liquid glistens in the sunlight and maybe you see a reflection of a bird flying overhead in a drop of suspended wine? And then the picture zooms in, becoming a garnet-colored ocean wave breaking over the crystal tip of the glass, now a sparkling ruby waterfall, cascading leisurely through the late summer afternoon breeze until it hits the woman's flowing, glossy blond hair and splashes onto her nose and rico-chets off her elegant cheekbones onto her décolletage and the front of her gown? And suddenly, after time has stood still and all the world has been reflected in those raindrops of wine, time speeds up to normal and she's sitting there, sopping wet with pink stains spoiling the front of her white dress? And we can see through her dress to her underwear and she's totally humiliated and hunched over, her soaked hair desperately gripping her skull?

This was kind of like that.

"And another thing," she screeched. "Stop interfering in my life. Stop texting my boyfriend for me, stop calling real-estate agents on my behalf, stop applying for jobs for me. You've got serious issues. If you've got to micro-manage something, get a fucking dog!"

My hands clutched the steering wheel. Thea had never said anything crude to me in her whole life. I mean, we swore at *stuff*, like traffic or the stapler when it got jammed or the garbage bag that split open as we took it out of the can, spilling old spaghetti sauce on the carpet. But not at each other. Never at each other.

Thea's eyes flamed with anger as she stared at me. Then she straightened up and slammed the door.

"Oh," I heard her say.

I couldn't drive away because Mr. Howard blocked my left, and I couldn't drive on the sidewalk on my right, even if I wanted to run over Thea, which in spite of my humilia-tion I did not. If the alien abduction wasn't going to happen, I wanted a violent summer thunderstorm to over-come us, strike me through the window, and render me a smoking heap of ash.

"I didn't see you," Thea said.

"Hi," said Mr. Howard.

"Well," Thea said. I could only see her through the window, from her knees to her chest. Her hands hovered in front of her, like any second now she'd strike up the band.

"Are you…the Delivery Guy?" she asked.

Mr. Howard didn't answer right away. I stared straight ahead at those stupid Grateful Dead dancing bears. They mocked me with their carefree grins. Out of the corner of my eye I saw Mr. Howard lift his hand. He held a white plastic bag; I could see the red printing on the white paper cartons through the thin plastic.

"I'm *a* delivery guy." He paused. "Did you order some food?"

"No," Thea said.

The dancing bears kicked off their crayon-hued parade across Mr. Howard's bumper. I saw one of them move, which was a clear sign that I'd lost my mind. I'll bet it ran away with my dignity.

"Well," Thea said again. Then she turned and jogged back up the steps and into her building.

Mr. Howard didn't say anything, but he didn't move, either.

Two months later, he spoke. "She seems nice," he said.

I nodded. But I felt tears falling for the umpteenth time today, and I wanted to get home.

Mr. Howard stepped back from the car. "I have a delivery I've got to make," he said, backing away like I might sink my claws into him if he turned to go. But honestly, if I could have transfigured him into a bird to expedite his departure, I wouldn't have hesitated.

"See you," he said over his shoulder as he slipped into the Toyota.

CHAPTER SIXTEEN

A nyone can embarrass you. A stranger can do it, like the check-out clerk at the drugstore announcing via loud speaker: "I need a price check on vaginal cream at register one." Or an acquaintance, like the nurse at the health clinic who reads your chart and remarks, "Wow, you've gained twelve pounds since your last visit." At a work meeting, a colleague might point out that the question you've asked is on the very topic the presenter just discussed, which you would have known except the presenter droned on like Ben Stein in *Ferris Bueller's Day Off* and put you to sleep. You can even embarrass yourself by, say, falling on your ass as you step out of an elevator in front of total strangers (not that I'd know), or by spending twenty minutes in conversation with someone and calling them the wrong name, repeatedly (again, nothing I'm familiar with). These are just examples. But true humiliation, the kind that lays you low, can only come from those you love best.

I went home and crawled into bed, even though it was midafternoon. Nothing good could come from the rest of this day. I took two Benadryls to make myself sleepy, but I napped in fits and starts. Every few hours I woke up, still as fretful and perplexed as I'd been in my car.

Despite the hours of time I spent in my own head, Thea knew me better than I knew myself. This wasn't the life I wanted—not professionally, not personally—and she called me on it. How did this all happen? I wanted answers, now.

The words came to me reflexively, drilled into my head from thirty-five years of repetition. "Be patient," Mom said to me anytime I demanded anything. I'd trusted in patience, in Mom's reassurance that all would turn out the way it was supposed to. What did that even mean, "supposed to?" I didn't believe in a micromanaging God, pushing people around like pawns on a cosmic chessboard.

But I'd trusted in patience. Patience, meanwhile, got soft on my couch, complacent. Inert, even. I'd become inert in my own observations. I couldn't see—or didn't want to see—what I'd become.

Thea knew, but was too kind even in her anger to say, that I wasn't thrilled with who I saw when I looked in the mirror. Deeper than my haircut, my clothing, or even my body.

Let's acknowledge that you can't keep your hands off my life because it's safer than tampering with your own. You're taking risks with my career because you're too scared to take them with yours.

I threw off my blanket and punched the air conditioner

to a cooler setting. God, it was stifling in here. As I climbed back into bed, I reached for my second bed pillow, searching for a cool spot.

What was I afraid of? Ha. Where to start?

I could fill a legal pad with a list of things I was afraid of: cockroaches, mugging, creeps on the subway. Contracting hepatitis from eating out of a street vendor's food cart, having my identity stolen. The biggest thing, though—hiding out at the bottom of the list, bookmarked for some other distant day's reflection—was that I was afraid to admit to myself that I was the one who'd put me here.

I hated my mind-numbing job. Though I'd spent years convincing myself otherwise, the generous retirement plan and full medical and dental insurance couldn't compensate for having to spend eight hours a day producing material I couldn't care less about. No matter how many vacation days I accrued, there weren't enough to make me refreshed and happy to return to the office, because there wasn't any love for the work to which I returned.

I had only myself to blame. I'd known when I graduated that the life I dreamed of wasn't to be found in DC, but the prospect of going after my dreams in New York left me retching into the toilet. An unfamiliar city, filled with unfamiliar people, no means of support, and family far away—it would have been too much change all at once. So I'd persuaded myself to believe that if I was patient, the happily-ever-after life I wanted would somehow come to me. I'd cheated myself out of professional fulfillment by staying where I was safe; where my days were predictable; where my friends and colleagues were known; where home, even if I didn't want to go back there, was just a few hours' car ride away.

If a friend proposed the same plan to me, I'd have told her, certain of my righteousness, that she'd set herself on a fool's errand. Life didn't come to you, friend, you had to make it happen. But I couldn't tell that to myself. Why? What was I really afraid of?

Failure, in a word. So many opportunities for failure. I was afraid to quit my job without another one lined up. A rational concern, for sure, but had I even looked around? No, because I might have found something. Then I'd have to take a chance on an unknown quantity, which might turn out to be worse than what I had now. On paper, it was hard to imagine anything being worse than *Recycling World*, but in my imagination, there were endless opportunities for regret.

I'd been afraid to move to New York and go after the career I really wanted—a literary editor; there, I said it—because the unknowns were too great. I'd been afraid I wouldn't find an apartment in a safe place or a job I could live on, afraid I'd have to ask my parents for money, and of the judgment that would accompany that request. That, with my lingering twangy accent, I'd never make friends. That I'd have to move back to Bishop's Creek, my tail between my legs, and take up residence in my old bedroom, reminded by the posters on the wall that I'd failed at Adulthood 101.

My personal life was equally miserable. How many conversations had Mom prefaced with, "When you've got a husband and children of your own…"? Not *if*, crucially, but *when*, conditioning me to assume this outcome, too, was inevitable. It never occurred to me that the *when* might not arrive. "You'll meet someone, probably when you go to college," she'd said. I'd kept my eyes open. I'd met lots of people. I'd gone to every party I could. Then, as I sat on the football field and turned my tassel, I pretended not to be concerned that her prophecy had gone unfulfilled. It's just around the corner, I told myself. Just be patient.

My fear was responsible for my personal life's equally disastrous condition. No shortage of opportunities for ugly failures there. I avoided putting myself in awkward situations, like clubs or blind dates, or even Mom's recommendation of church, because I'd felt sure I'd only meet guys like Keith.

Who, as long as I'm telling the truth here, had nothing wrong with him besides the fact that he was a lonely guy looking for someone to be with. Socially unpolished? Sure. Terrified of rejection? Who isn't?

But really, that wasn't the problem. It wasn't the ickiness of the situation that put me off, not the series of underwhelming dates that would inevitably follow. No, I was afraid that I'd be a female Keith, too awkward to be chosen, too lonely to be worthwhile. There must be a reason that, at this age, I was still on the market, right?

Telling myself online dating was a tool of last resort, I put my faith in that slob, patience. If I held out long enough, I would meet someone organically. Here again, I'd relied on Thea, who did put herself out there. Any time she met a new guy, I responded, "Oh, he sounds wonderful. Does he have a friend for me?" I'd practically tattooed the words on my tongue. And in the absence of anyone else, I'd depended on Thea, my dear friend, to fill the space in my heart that demanded I matter to someone.

Someone else, that is. If no one else materialized, could I cope with that? Could I be happy alone? Did I matter to me?

I got up and stumbled to the kitchen. I filled a tall glass with ice, topped it off with water, gulped the water down, and dumped the ice in the sink. I stared at the cubes there, reflected streetlight casting a sheen over their melting tops.

Without a job I cared about, and without a family who cared about me, who was I, after all? If I had to fill out a profile for a cosmic online dating service that would help me find my soul mate, my dearest and most faithful friends, or my perfect vocation, could I produce a compelling narrative? Would I have a hero's journey, or would I remain marginal even in my own biography? Could I analyze the character of Jane, protagonist in my own life's story? I knew her tragic flaw, but could I identify any redeeming traits that would help her triumph in the end?

It was a heavy question for three a.m., or for any time of day. I knew the short answer to the question: No, I couldn't. But it was clear to me, even at that confused early hour, that I needed to find a better answer, and it wouldn't be a quick study.

I filled my glass with more water, no ice, and drank it slowly. Staring out the window over the sink into the darkened windows of the apartments down the block, I wondered who else might be up at this hour, and what they were thinking.

I drained the glass and curled up on the sofa, pulling a

blanket off the top of the laundry basket nearby. As the soft cotton caressed my bare feet, I thought of Sam, huddled in the doorway of the bank. Was I afraid of that fate? For Thea or for me?

No, not really. Even if worse came to worst for Thea, that would mean going home to Bishop's Creek, getting dragged down into a life where opportunities dwindled by the day. But she'd never let it come to that. She had too much grit, too much fierce belief in herself to let that happen. She'd keep fighting, smarter and smarter, until she got herself where she wanted to be.

I didn't fear it for me, either. I wouldn't end up like Sam, subjected to the contempt of the suit-clad customers who stepped over me as if I were dog refuse left on the sidewalk. Even if I didn't want to go back home again, I had a network that wouldn't leave me on the street. I had people to fall back on.

That thought made me feel a little better. I wiped my eyes on the blanket, and my gaze fell on the basket of unfolded laundry that had yielded it up.

And beyond the basket, the mismatched worn hand-me-down furniture crouched in the dark, the same shapes I'd stumbled around all my life. Next to them, the dirty laundry, the piles of mail waiting to be recycled; over there, the dishes in the sink. In the closets and corners, dozens of plastic organizational systems, not performing as intended, serving instead as receptacles for undealt-with rubbish.

Jesus. What was the matter with me? I was thirty-five years old, and I still lived like an eighteen-year-old boy in his first college apartment.

Sam would have done better by this space, and I should have done better. Here I sat, patting my plump, well-tended hand for comfort, congratulating myself on my network that would protect me from the worst I could imagine. I didn't deserve that safety net. Thea wouldn't fall back on hers; I'd get tangled in mine. All this time I'd thought I was being kind, checking in on the homeless guy, but it wasn't honest concern. I didn't honor him by treating my own home, or my life, without any respect.

Maybe I didn't know who I was, but I was through hiding from myself. What lay in front of me? I had no idea. It would almost surely be uncomfortable, probably embarrassing. Could it be humiliating? I wasn't sure. After all, that answer could only come from someone who knew and loved me best, and all evidence pointed clearly to the conclusion that that person was not me.

CHAPTER SEVENTEEN

My howling stomach woke me up, whining to be fed. As I stretched my cramped legs, my foot rammed the arm of the sofa. I rubbed my face. Why had I slept on the sofa?

Oh. Right.

The clock on the coffeemaker read 11:20, but my body argued it was the crack of dawn. In the kitchen, I made a pot of full-caffeine coffee. I grabbed a bowl but stopped pouring the Lucky Charms midstream. I deserved better than this. If my apartment, my self-image, and my life were all a mess, a box of sugared kids cereal was not going to propel me in a new and better direction.

I opened the door to pick up the paper and saw Dina and Rafael running races down the hall.

"Hey, Dina," I said as she zipped past me. She turned. "Do you like Lucky Charms?"

"Yeah!" she said.

"Wait right there." I retrieved the box and handed it to

her. "Here. Share it with Rafael, though. Tell your mom where you got it."

Rafael sprinted to her and plunged his hands into the box. I retrieved my paper, turned, and shut the door behind me.

If my life to date were a novel, it would be a cheap airport paperback with an uninspired cover, containing flat characters and a predictable plot. I'd read it too many times; it had nothing to teach me anymore. I needed to start a new, more challenging story.

I poured a cup of coffee and took a carton of eggs out of the refrigerator. I scrambled up two, and tossed in a handful of chopped herbs, tomatoes, peppers, and cheese. I plated my omelette, cleared the junk off my table, and set a place for one.

After breakfast, I washed and dried all the dishes and put them away. Then I went to my room, changed my sheets, and made my bed. I dressed in grubby clothes, tied my hair back, and grabbed a roll of garbage bags.

For the next five hours, I went through the piles of unsorted mail and cleaned out the boxes of clutter that I'd allowed to accumulate. If it was older than a year or if I'd forgotten about it, it went in the trash or the recycling. *Adios*, college econ notes! Fare thee well, three-year-old issues of *InStyle*. When I filled the first two bags, I took them down the hall to the garbage chute and dropped them in. I knew if I didn't do it immediately, I might second-guess myself and open them up, and with them, open up my old life.

I folded my clothes and put them away, then dusted every surface in the house. I scrubbed my bathroom until I could see a vague reflection on the wall of the porcelain tub.

Mindless cleaning, it turned out, cleaned the clutter from my mind, or at least it made a healthy start. I might not have all the answers yet, but I did have one. And I was ready to trust myself with it.

When I took the job at *Recycling World*—no, even further back, when I chose to move to DC—I promised myself that I'd use the time to gain skills and save money as I paid back my student loans. When the time was right, I'd look for something I genuinely wanted. "I'll know," I told my career counselor, who looked at me over the top of her glasses with the skepticism learned from years of watching her clients chicken out. I'd know when the time came to move on, although I assumed "the time" would come as a result of marriage and children, not identity crisis.

Now, more than a decade on, I'd been promoted twice. I had marketable skills and experience.

I had two student loan payments left to go. Staying in this apartment had been part of the promise: a tight squeeze into a tiny apartment would give me just enough independence while getting out of debt.

So it turns out, I was right. I did know the time to move on when it came. It was as bright and ugly as a fresh scar, and just as unmistakeable.

On Monday, I stopped into an office supply store on the way to work and bought a heavy-duty cardboard banker's box. Once inside my office, I turned on the computer and printed out the letter I'd drafted the night before.

I knocked on Cliff's office door. When he grunted, "Come in," I took a deep breath (more to guard against the aroma than to steel my nerves), and walked in.

"Good morning, Cliff. I've done some thinking, and it's time for me to move on. Here's my letter of resignation; my last day will be a week from Friday."

Cliff looked up in confusion from his computer screen. His eyes were bloodshot and glassy behind his bifocal frames.

"What? You're quitting? Why?"

"This has been a great place to work. I've learned so much. But I've been here thirteen years, and it's time I moved on to different subject matter, different challenges."

Cliff scanned the letter, sat back in his chair, and looked up at me.

"Huh. You know, I'd pegged you as a lifer. I figured I'd hand the reins over to you when I retired."

Even he had seen surrender in me. No matter; I saw it now. "I appreciate the compliment, Cliff. But I think it's better this way."

"Where are you going?"

"New York, I think." It hadn't been real in my mind until then, but I saw myself driving over the Brooklyn Bridge, my car packed to the gills. "I don't have anything lined up at the moment."

"Biological clock ticking?"

"What?! No. That has nothing to do with it."

Cliff shrugged.

"I've got things I need to wrap up," I said. "I'll look at

your calendar and suggest some times we can meet as I prepare to leave."

Cliff nodded, his attention already wandering to the stack of equipment photos on his desk. I closed the door behind me and turned down the hall, inhaling a fresh new breath that was all the more exhilarating because it left behind the aroma of stale fried onions, the stench of self-compromise.

———

I'd never worked with such focus in my life. I shucked off the monthly columns and the calendar to Sarah, the intern. I emailed all my scheduled appointments for the next month, announcing my imminent departure and referring them to Cliff. I canceled my conference registrations and deleted miles of archived emails. I got forms from HR to roll over my 401(k) to a private retirement account. Every task that drew my employment closer to closure felt like five pounds of weight lifted from my back.

That afternoon, Keith dropped by. "Desmond. I heard you're quitting."

"That's right," I sang. Hearing his verbal confirmation of my decision felt like a vote of confidence in me. It thrilled me so much, I didn't even mind him settling into my guest chair to visit.

"You're going to New York?"

"That's the plan." As if I had a plan. The words just came out.

"But you don't have a job there yet?"

"You've gathered a lot of information about me," I observed.

"I'm surprised," he said. "You seemed happy here."

"Did I?"

"Weren't you?"

The cautious part of me started sending semaphore signals: He's not discreet; don't burn bridges. "Well, of course, it's a good company," I said. "A fine place to work. I just need a change of scenery."

Keith drew a cheap ballpoint pen from his pocket. He removed the cap, then replaced it. He twirled it in his fingers like a tiny baton. Hoping to postpone whatever he might say next, I assembled the banker's box and dumped the bottom drawer of my desk into it. Spare clothes, old makeup, paperbacks I'd bought but hadn't yet read.

"I'll miss you," he said.

"Thanks, Keith." Buoyed by the prospect of better days ahead, I felt generous. "I'll miss you, too."

"Want to grab a good-bye drink?"

He looked so pathetic, sitting in my guest chair and twisting the cap on the pen. Now that this place was behind me, I couldn't believe how much energy I'd invested in hiding from him. He was just a sad, lonely guy, a male version of me. Neither one of us was unworthy. But I was done hiding from truth.

"Keith, it's a kind offer, but no. I hope you find someone who treats you well and makes you happy. But that someone is not destined to be me."

He pushed himself from his chair and scratched his stomach.

"Well, I guess that's that, then," he said. "Listen, do you know if Sarah's—"

"She's a lesbian," I said, unsure if that was true but wanting to put all the distance between them I could, for her sake.

"All the time?" he asked.

"Yes. And I think she's engaged, too."

He nodded slowly. "See you," he said and slipped out the door, drumming his hand on the wall as he went.

On that final Friday, the staffs of *Recycling World, Cement World*, and *Dust Suppression Monthly* came to the conference room to eat sheet cake on my behalf. They'd all signed a card wishing me well. Inside was a gift certificate to the Strand Bookstore in Manhattan for $200.

"We know you like to read," Cliff offered. After thirteen years, that was all they knew about me.

"Wow," I said, genuinely surprised. "Thank you very much. I'll try not to blow it all in one visit."

"Maybe we'll come into the city and see you next time the Waste Expo is in Newark," he said.

Not if I see you first, I thought. But caution pulled rank over my dedication to truth, this time. "I can't wait," I said.

CHAPTER EIGHTEEN

Quitting my job was the easy part. Telling my mom to quit interfering in my life? An entirely different prospect.

I paced around my living room—something I could actually do, now that I'd cleaned house—and practiced conversations with her in my head. Could I avoid hurting her feelings? How best to approach the conversation, to make it stick?

I could hear her now: "I just want you to be happy, honey." Her motives were genuine and kindly intended. But I needed her to see that her definition of happiness might not be the same as mine. I didn't know. I had to figure mine out first.

I picked up the phone and found her contact number three times, and three times I set the phone down. Why did confrontation have to be so ugly? But I couldn't run away from it, and I couldn't get around it. No, the only way out was through. Like Churchill said.

I grabbed a shot glass from the cabinet, poured a shot of gin, because that's what I had, and pounded it down. I don't recommend this tactic, by the way, but doing it persuaded me I could tackle this challenge, so I pounded another just in case. Then I washed and dried the glass, put it back in the cabinet, picked up the phone, and called her.

"Hello, darling," Mom said. "I was getting ready to call you. I hadn't heard from you in a while. How's your week been?"

Refusing to let small talk kill my momentum, I launched myself into the fray. "It's been dramatic," I said.

"Dramatic?" I could hear her rustling papers in the background.

"In a good way. Well, sort of. It's going to be good. But it's ugly right now."

"Poor dear. Tell me all about it."

"Well. I had a major fight with Thea, and she's not speaking to me, and rightfully so. I had met someone I thought might be a romantic prospect, but he witnessed the fight with Thea so he thinks I'm insane, so that's unsalvageable. I realized I hate my job, and it's my fault I hate my job, so I quit. And I've decided to get out of this apartment and move to New York. How's that for drama?"

The paper rustling on the other end of the line stopped abruptly. "Say all that again?"

"I had a fight with Thea, I killed my budding romantic relationship, I quit my job, and I gave notice to vacate my apartment."

On the other end, I heard a chair scrape across the floor.

She was sitting down at the kitchen table. "Sugar, have you lost your mind?"

"Nope," I said, feeling vigorous. "I've found it."

"Do you have a new job in New York?"

"No."

"Do you know anyone there?"

"No."

"Do you have a place to live?"

"Not yet."

She exhaled. "I wish your father was here. He went to play tennis. Honey, lots of people have a midlife crisis—"

"I'm not having a midlife crisis, Mom." The rule was you had to be at least forty to have a midlife crisis. I had five years to go.

"It sounds like a midlife crisis. All that's missing is a new convertible and a family to leave behind. Thank God you can't do that."

"That's the first time I've ever heard you say you're glad I'm not attached."

"Look, Jane, whatever's going on with Thea, if that's what's behind all this, it will get sorted out. You've been friends for too long. You don't have to quit your job and move away."

"Mom, it's not just the fight with Thea."

"Did you get fired?"

"No, of course not. I quit."

"I thought you loved that job. Working all those late hours and so on."

"I lied about that. I never loved that job. I was good at it, but it was never what I wanted."

"I can't believe you're going to pick up and move to

someplace where you know absolutely no one and you don't have a job. If that's not a midlife crisis, I don't know what is."

It was a lot for her to take in, so I let her absorb it. I grabbed a dust cloth from the cupboard and dusted the furniture as I waited for her to speak.

"Jane? Are you still there?"

"Yes, I'm still here."

"So. Well." I could hear her fidgeting in the background, scraping her chair forward and back on the hard floor. "When…when do you have to move out? Do you need me to come with you to New York and help you find someplace to live?"

"No, I don't. I'm thirty-five. I can do this on my own."

She held her breath for a moment, then let it out. It sounded like she was surfacing from a long, deep underwater dive.

"I…I don't know what to say. I'm just stunned, Jane. This isn't like you, to be so drastic."

"Well, I think that's part of the problem, actually. I've been too cautious for too long. It's time I took some risks. My anxiety got the better of me for too long, and now I feel like I've sold myself short."

"Is this about the boyfriend? Was it Paul Alexander? You never mentioned—"

"No, I never mentioned. And it's not about him. I never called Paul Alexander, and he never called me. Because neither one of us wanted to be set up. This is all about me. That's what you need to understand."

"Are you going to New York because you met someone there?"

"No, I'm not following anyone there. I'm not attached, and I'm not even close. I'm moving all on my own, because I want to."

"Jane, this makes no sense. I don't think you've thought this through."

"Well, you're right that I haven't made a detailed plan. When I graduated from college, I wanted to move to New York, but I was scared. I talked myself out of it. I settled for a job I didn't want, and I tried to pretend its security made up for its tedium. But it didn't. I've been too safe all my life. I'm not even really out of your nest, to be honest. It's time I pushed myself out there and tried to fly on my own."

"It's a big change, Jane. Bigger than you think."

"I hope so."

"Let me at least call around, see if I can get some contacts for you. I think Donna Grimes's son lives in New York. He's a banker of some kind. He can—"

"NO!" I screamed. "Are you listening to a word I'm saying? I need to do this on my own. I don't want your help. I don't want you coming to New York to pick out an apartment for me, I don't want you second-guessing my decisions, I don't want you gathering phone numbers for me, and I definitely don't want you calling your friends' sons to fix me up."

"I'm only trying to help—"

"Yes, but you're not helping. You're hurting. I've begged you to stop interfering, but you never listen to me. You don't believe that I might have my own ideas about my own happiness. You still think that mother knows best. Well, you don't know better than I do what I want for my career, or for my personal life, or for my own happiness. You just don't. And I want you to stop trying to fix things for me. I want you to leave me alone."

The words just came out.

I heard her choke on the other end of the phone. I didn't mean to be quite so harsh about it. Was it the gin shots? Or was it simply Jane, finding herself? A college friend once told me, after I'd made a fool of myself at a party, "Alcohol doesn't make you into a different person, Jane. Alcohol just makes you more you." And who are we kidding? It hadn't even hit my bloodstream yet. This was me. Pure, angry me.

Mom sniffled. Her mouth made a smacking sound, the one that happens when your tongue fills up your dry mouth and you can't swallow, and all your face moisture is leaking from your eyes and nose instead of staying in your mouth where it belongs.

"Mom, don't cry."

"Don't you think I deserve a little cry? My own daughter doesn't want me involved in her life."

Oh God, here came the guilt, her most formidable weapon. Would I let it cut me off at the knees? Keep going, I told myself. Fight smarter. Fight for yourself.

"Mom, let's see the nuance here. I don't want you out of my life entirely. I want to be friends with you. I want you to treat me as a grown-up. That means stop trying to fix my problems. I can find my own place to live. I can find my own job. I can find my own partner, if I want one. I can find my own happiness."

She sobbed.

"We can still talk. You can come to New York and visit

me when I'm ready. But not before I'm ready. I'm going to set limits, and I'm going to enforce them. I have to.

"We can only be on good terms if they're different terms from now on. You need to respect my independence. I need to respect my independence, too. I need to be clear when stuff's not helping.

"All these people you try to fix me up with," I said. "Don't you think I might want to pick someone out for myself?"

"I don't want you to be lonely," she said.

"I think," I said, surprised at the truth that tumbled out of my mouth, "I think it would be good for me to be lonely. For a while. I've always assumed I would have a family, but the truth is, it might not happen. You might not get any grandkids. You can't push it on me to make it happen. You need to let that go. If it happens, it happens. If not, oh, well.

"It's a novel idea to me, to be honest with you. Lots of things haven't panned out the way I expected them to. I need to get happy with myself and my own life. Because whether or not I find someone else, I'm going to be with myself the rest of my life. I need to figure out who I am apart from my job and apart from a family. I need to figure out me."

Mom blew her nose.

"Mom?"

"Yes?"

"Are you with me?"

She didn't answer right away. The chair creaked, and she sighed as she shifted in her seat. I waited.

"I guess if that's really what you want...but this

running off to find yourself, it sounds like you've lost your mind. I think once your father gets home we'll call you back."

"He can call if he wants, but he won't change my mind."

"I don't understand, Jane, I don't. I only ever tried to help."

"I know you did. But you didn't ask whether I wanted your help."

"A mother can't stop worrying about her child. One day you'll—" She stopped herself. Maybe something had gotten through to her.

"I might understand one day, or I might not," I said. "Either way, you raised me to be independent. Think of it like this. For the past thirteen years, I've been riding on my own, but with training wheels. I've got the hang of it now, and it's time to take off the training wheels. I can go further on my own. I don't need you running behind me to catch me. If I fall down, I'll get up by myself. I don't need someone else there. I just need me."

The sniffles had smoothed out, except for a little one here or there. Although she was quiet, her breathing had returned to a regular pattern. Inhale, exhale.

I did it.

"Are you okay?" I asked her.

"I need to call your father."

"Okay. But don't try and stage an intervention."

"Will you stop it? I get it, okay? You don't want us involved."

"Mom, I'm saying it's got to be different. Not out of my life entirely, but it's not your life to manage."

"I only know one way to be your mother," she snapped.

"Well, maybe I can teach you another."

"I doubt it. There are some things only a mother can understand."

"That may be true," I acknowledged. "But I always thought I could count on your support. Growing up, you always said you'd support me, no matter what."

"That was before you started making idiotic choices."

I took a breath. One more tug and I'd be through.

"I love you, Mom. But you can't talk to me that way anymore. I'll let you know when I get settled in New York. Good-bye." And I hung up the phone.

CHAPTER NINETEEN

L eaving *Recycling World* was easy. Telling Mom to butt out was difficult. Breaking up with my best friend of the past twenty-five years? This might be the hardest task of them all.

It probably wouldn't be forever, I told myself, only until I get my head on straight. But in fairness to her—and, I suppose, to myself as well—it needed to happen for a little while.

It wasn't lost on me that yet again, I was following in Thea's footsteps. Sure, she'd been forced onto her new path ahead of her plan, whereas I had thrown myself out on my own accord. But just as she'd decided to pursue the life she'd always envisioned, so, too, did I intend to grab the world by the throat. Assuming, of course, it didn't grab me first.

At home, I made my last student loan payment. I took a screenshot to commemorate the event. The end of one phase, the beginning of another. Then, at my newly tidied desk in the corner of my bedroom, I sat down to write a letter.

Dear Thea,

Before you use this letter to light your inaugural grill fire, let me promise that this is the last you'll hear from me for a while. I've owed you this letter for a long time now, and that delay is yet another thing for which I must apologize.

Not that you need a recap, but I want to make sure I'm comprehensive in case I've screwed up our friendship beyond repair: I tried to find you a job, and I tried to fix your life. You asked for neither of these interventions, but that didn't stop me, and I am sorry. If I'd used any imagination, I might have realized that I was treating you exactly the way my mother treats me. Knowing that I'm turning into my mother is, I assure you, adequate punishment here in my ninth circle of personal hell. Is it cold in here, or is it just me?

You are, as usual, right that I was too fearful to take risks in my own life, so I meddled in yours to compensate. I don't deserve to be forgiven, but I hope in time you will. I truly am sorry.

Furthermore, I'm sorry for everything I said and did when I pretended to know what was in your best interests. I'm sorry I didn't listen to you, or support you in a way that was actually, you know, supportive. I'm sorry I let you down when you needed someone.

And while I'm cataloging all the ways I abused our friendship and sucked you dry, let me also say I was wrong to depend on you for my social life. That wasn't fair. I never intended to smother you, but of course, I assumed my good intention would be clear to you simply because it was clear in my own muddled head. I put my needs, ideas, and anxieties ahead of yours—even ahead of your joys. I took a lot, I gave little in return, and I'm sorry for that, too. No wonder you wanted to move away. Who could blame you?

I've always admired you, you know. When you were laid off, you could have panicked and taken the first thing you could find, continuing in a career that paid your bills but didn't inspire you. Instead, you made a bold move to pursue something new. I know that whatever it is you're planning, you'll succeed brilliantly. You always do. I don't know what you're cooking up because you warned Narin not to tell me, which was, again, a good decision on your part. You know me better than I know myself. But I hope that will change.

I'm taking my cues from you one last time. In a few weeks, I'm moving to New York. I've already quit my job at Recycling World. My last day was yesterday. I have nothing here to tide me over, nor do I have anything waiting for me in New York. Doesn't sound like me, does it? Well, maybe the old me isn't actually me. The old me is the person I became by default, because I was scared to trust myself.

Who knows whether it will work out? At least I'll be able to say I gave it a try.

If you'd like to get together for a farewell beer before I go, you know where to find me. If not, maybe I'll see you back in Bishop's Creek at Christmas, assuming Mom recovers from the heart attack I gave her when I broke the news, and that she lets me back into her house.

I hope you can forgive me for being such a parasite. You'll always be my favorite friend. Lucky you.

Love,

Jane

My building is an older one, built between the world wars, and on every floor there's a mail chute with a glass front so you can watch your letter commence its postal journey. Somewhere downstairs it all collects in a giant mailbox. When I first moved in, I was skeptical whether anyone would still use it, or whether the mail was collected from wherever it went. But every day I saw people dropping letters in, so I started using it. It's one of my favorite things about living here, that old-fashioned mail chute.

Calm, or maybe it was simply fatigue, washed over me as I finished the letter, folded it, and put it in an envelope I addressed to Thea. I fixed a stamp on one corner and scribbled my return address in the other. I padded down the hall in my stockinged feet to the mail chute. As I stood there, a letter fluttered past, twirling down the glass-fronted niche in the wall like an oversized maple seed.

Before I could change my mind, I seized the handle of the chute opening, dropped my letter to Thea inside, and slammed the door. My letter plunged straight down, gone almost before I could step back to look.

Nearly a week later, on Thursday, I was coming out of my building's leasing office when Thea's ringtone trilled on my phone.

I'd just finished making arrangements to sublet my apartment until my lease ran out. It would save me a bundle, cash I could certainly use as I tried to figure out how on earth I was going to make my way in New York. My hands shook as I tried to slide the bar to answer the call.

"Hello?" I asked, halfway certain it would be the police or a paramedic, telling me they'd found my name in Thea's phone as an emergency contact.

"Hey, it's me," came Thea's voice.

"Hi." I pushed open the building's heavy front door and sat on a bench under a tree.

"I got your letter."

"Yeah? I wasn't sure you'd read it once you recognized my handwriting and the return address."

"I didn't read it, not right away. Actually, my dad told me you were going to New York, and I thought that wasn't right. That got me thinking about the letter, and I asked Narin to read it first and tell me whether I should read it myself."

"Caution is a smart thing to practice. Especially when I'm involved."

"So you're going to New York, huh? For real?"

"Every day it looks more and more like it. I just signed papers to sublet my apartment."

"Wow. You're really doing it."

"Yeah. So I'd better get my butt up there and find myself a place to land."

"Are you nervous?"

"Yes. But I'm hopeful. Whatever's ahead, it's better than what I'm leaving behind. I mean, besides you."

She was quiet. "That's fantastic, Jane. I'm really happy for you."

"Thanks."

"I mean it. I will miss you, for sure. It'll be weird, not being able to see you any old time. Not being able to run up the street to grab Chinese with you."

"Well, now that you've moved, we can't do that anyway."

"But you're still close."

"Was I right? Did you move to get away from me?"

Thea hesitated. "Not exactly. No. I wanted to feel more permanent. I'd been in the apartment for six years, and in the District for thirteen. I wanted a space of my own, something that would feel like mine. Maybe I wanted a little more independence, but not..."

"A divorce?" I asked.

She laughed. "Definitely not that. It might feel like it now, since you'll be so far away. What prompted all of this?"

"Do you have to ask?"

She paused. "I'm sorry I was so hateful that day."

"You had a right to be."

"Assertive, maybe, but not hateful. Did all that really make you pick up and leave?"

"It made me think. That was something I hadn't done much of lately. I've been on autopilot. That's no way to go through life."

"Can I come see you?"

"Of course. That is, assuming I find a place to live where I don't have to sleep standing up."

"It's a long way from Bishop's Creek."

"Yes, that's one of its charms."

"Dad said your mom lost it when you told her."

"She did. I guess she'll never stop worrying about me."

"Did she ask if you were going after a guy?"

"Naturally."

"And?"

"No."

"Just thought I'd ask." She was quiet for a moment. "Listen, I did read your letter. Do you want to get together for a good-bye drink?"

"Yes."

"Why don't you come out to my house? We'll have dinner, and you can see it, now that it's all fixed up."

"That sounds wonderful."

"I'll see you tomorrow at six."

CHAPTER TWENTY

At 6:20, I climbed the steps to Thea's townhouse. Pots of succulents adorned the steps, and cartoon dogs frolicked on the welcome mat. I rang the bell. Moments later, footsteps beat a tattoo down the hardwood floor, a crescendo that matched my heartbeat and ended with the clear metallic click of the door's lock.

"Hi, Jane," Thea said. She greeted me the way you might greet a professional colleague you'd met once at a training seminar six months before, warm but with reserve. No remark about Jane time, either. "Come on in."

She stepped back to let me enter. Her furniture was arranged thoughtfully, pictures hung with precision. Books and photographs and decorative objects stood aligned on end tables and shelves with a set decorator's finesse. It didn't look like a house being lived in; it looked like a house ready to be put on the market.

Cleo crept out from behind a chair and wound herself around my legs. I reached down to scratch her ears.

"It's been a long time, hasn't it, Cleo?" I asked her.

"Let's sit on the screened porch," Thea said. "It's not awful outside today."

She led me through the kitchen and family room to the back porch, where two generous patio chairs flanked a glass-topped iron table. "What can I get you?" she asked me.

I shrugged. "Whatever's fine." To make a specific request felt impertinent.

Thea disappeared into the kitchen as I sat back in the deep cushions of the chair. Cleo leapt into my lap. I stroked her back as she kneaded my thighs, "making biscuits," as Mr. Willis used to call it. She turned around and flicked her tail, then settled in for a nap.

Thea came back with two beers and smiled at Cleo. "She's missed you, I think," she said, handing me a sweating brown bottle. "She got used to you coming by every day."

"I missed her, too."

"Thanks for taking care of her."

"It was my pleasure."

Thea settled into the chair opposite me.

"Your place looks great."

"Thanks. It's been fun putting it together."

She looked happy and relaxed. The dark circles that usually hung beneath her eyes had disappeared, and the parallel tracks of lines in her forehead had smoothed out. She took a long pull from her beer and watched me. I watched her in return.

"So. New York."

I nodded. "New York."

"That's a big change."

"It is," I agreed.

I stroked Cleo's back. Did Thea expect me to grovel more? I was genuinely sorry, but I'd said what I had to say in the letter. Perhaps this what our relationship would feel like from now on, like a pair of shoes that once fit but for some reason—built-up calluses, a broken toe—no longer did.

"When do you leave?" she asked.

"Next week."

"Where will you live? Do you have a place yet?"

"No. I've got an Airbnb place I'm renting for a month, and I'll figure it out from there."

"And no job?"

The more she questioned me, the more foolish I felt. What had I been thinking? Pick up and move to one of the most expensive cities in the world with no job and no contacts? How was I going to find a place to live if I couldn't prove I could pay rent?

Still, when I left *Recycling World* with my banker's box under my arm, my Strand gift certificate tucked safely inside, and a foil-wrapped block of going-away cake balanced on top of it all, my internal compass pointed due north for the first time. Every image of me slogging through Midtown crowds or reading manuscripts on the subway sent thrills of electricity down my spine.

I shook my head. "No job."

Thea whistled. "You've got more guts than I have, Jane Desmond."

Did I? When I packed boxes or stashed furniture in my newly rented storage unit in Bethesda, I believed in myself. Every box I sealed up, every bag of garbage I disposed of, every piece of old clothing I took to the thrift store, lifted weight from me. It wasn't even metaphorical; whether it came from schlepping boxes or from some dopamine surge in my system, I'd lost five pounds. Like an archaeologist brushing away layer over layer of dirt, the traces of myself were becoming clearer and clearer. There was an outline now, a detectable shape. Something to work toward, carefully and slowly.

But whenever someone spoke the terms of my plan aloud, every argument I had for my decision vaporized, just like the excuses I'd prepared to ward off Keith's attentions. I resorted to plastering on a grimace and offering a feeble joke about a midlife crisis.

How can you rationalize something to someone when all evidence points to a long shot, but your heart knows it's a sure bet?

A few years ago they found the skeleton of King Richard III under a city parking lot in Leicester, in central England. The people supporting the project had done historical research, assessed the site with radar, raised money, tried to persuade everyone they were on to something. One of the main advocates was a historian, a woman whose name escapes me. She aimed to debunk centuries of myth surrounding the king. He didn't have a withered arm; he didn't have a hunchback. She'd prove the truth: Shakespeare, that Tudor shill, had slandered Richard and wrecked his reputation. They were granted permission to excavate a couple of trenches, each about five feet wide and one hundred feet long—a splinter's worth of space.

Naturally, if you announce you're hoping to dig up a parking lot to find a king who's been dead five hundred years, someone's going to second-guess your decisions. They might even question your intelligence; I mean, taking away someone's off-street parking won't win you any allies. Even the most supportive folk will remind you to be realistic and check yourself: say you're hoping to find a trace of the ancient church rather than the bones of a king. Be cautious. Don't put your hopes out there.

But that woman believed. With half the archaeology team rolling their eyes at her hunches and biting their tongues at her theories, she persisted. And damned if they didn't dig up the king's leg bones on the very first day.

"So, has your mom gotten over the shock yet?" Thea asked, pulling my thoughts back to the present.

"Good question."

"I mean, it's been almost two weeks now, right?"

"I don't know," I said. "I haven't talked to her."

At some point, the historian probably had doubted herself. I mean, I don't know a woman who doesn't doubt herself for half her waking hours. But once the backhoes came in, she couldn't fake indifference. I don't know how she did it, how she reconciled herself to the idea that, in the long run, trusting herself outweighed the risk of humiliation. Did she know then that she'd have to be her strongest ally? Did she remind herself, even on days when she didn't believe it, that if she was faithful she'd find what she sought. Not just bones, but truth? All I know is she made the only move she could make with integrity. She pushed her chips to the center of the table and laid down her hand: I'm all in, world. Show me what you've got.

The label on my beer bottle curled back onto itself on one corner, so I scraped at it, nudging the paper into my palm with my thumbnail.

"You know that peeling a beer label is supposed to be a sign of sexual frustration," Thea teased.

If I hadn't taken a wrecking ball to my friendship with Thea by interfering in her job search, would it still have crumbled, just in some other way? Maybe my incessant hammering at her to set me up with someone or my curiosity about her new job venture would have chipped away at it. My needs might have fallen into the spaces between us, packing tighter and tighter and forcing us apart, until I buried us in my own personal rubble.

I lifted my glance from the beer bottle up to her face. "Well, I suppose those jokes exist for a reason."

Thea bit her lip. "You never talked to the delivery guy again, did you?"

I shook my head.

"I shouldn't—"

"Forget it," I said. "It's behind me."

It must have been thrilling for that woman who believed, to watch the excavators crack through the compacted tar and gravel to the soft earth below. There's a fine line, though, between thrilling and sickening. Did the butterflies in her stomach rise up her throat to hover in the back of her mouth, the way mine did these days?

"It's going to be so strange, your not being close by," Thea said. "I know I said that the other day, but I still can't get my head around it. I feel like I have phantom-limb syndrome already, you know? Like my right arm feels like it's there, but when I look down, it's gone."

"I'm glad you think of me as a limb," I said. "As opposed to, say, a tumor."

"Don't be ridiculous," she said, rolling her eyes. She watched me cuddle Cleo. "Aren't you scared? I don't think I could pull it off without either the job or the apartment in place. I'd be terrified if I were you."

I shrugged and pulled out my plastic grin.

"I can't get over it," she continued, shaking her head. "Seriously, when I heard the doorbell I considered opening the door and saying, 'Who are you and what have you done with my best friend?'"

The historian recognized him in the deformed curve of his spine, where ancient myth tangled with modern truth. But here's the crazy thing: at the moment she knew she'd triumphed, she also believed she failed. She aimed to disprove the grotesque legends and what told her she'd found him? That curved back of his.

Maybe she took comfort in knowing she'd pulled off the impossible. Maybe she kept it together until she got home, where she locked the door, drew the blinds, threw her shoes at the wall, and screamed every four-letter word in the book. Maybe it took a long soak in a hot bath for her to remember that she hadn't closed the book on him; no way, she'd just cracked it open.

She'd lived and breathed and slept the subject, but even she had more to learn about him. He was no longer myth and history; he was real, and ready to be understood.

Have patience.

Then came the tests, the carbon dating and the dietary analysis and the DNA sequencing of the ancient bones and the living descendants that proved it all beyond doubt.

It turned out to be scoliosis, not a hunchback. The famous portrait of the king wasn't wrong, but the myth of the monster was. I guess a lot of life is like that: There's truth hiding in the stories that get told to ourselves and to others, but the stories get out of hand sometimes. They get exaggerated, and we lose sight of what the truth is. We have to keep uncovering it, dusting it off so it doesn't get obscured by time and carelessness, so we don't forget what it looks like.

Nobody remembers that she tried and failed to disprove a myth. What they remember is that she found the truth. When she called the hand, she held the high card. A king, as fate would have it.

I finished my beer and set it on the end table. "Thanks, Thea. It was nice to visit with you and to see your place. But I need to get back. I've got more clearing out to do."

"Oh. I thought you'd stay longer. I have dinner in the oven—"

"I think I'd better go," I said, picking Cleo up in my arms and rising to my feet.

"If that's what you need." She followed me.

I nuzzled Cleo and leaned down to pick up the bottle. "I'll take care of that," she said, taking it from me and setting it on the counter.

I carried Cleo to the front door, hanging on to her softness as long as I could. "Don't worry, I'm not going to steal your cat," I said to Thea through a faceful of fur. Cleo stretched her paws and turned her head to look at me.

I stroked her cheek, then handed her over to Thea. She leapt from Thea's arms onto the back of a chair and squatted there, her tail curled around her body.

"Well, good luck," Thea said, opening her arms to me.

"Thanks," I said, returning the hug. "Good luck to you, too."

Her mouth twisted in a grin. "Did Narin tell you what I'm doing? Do you even know?"

"I don't," I admitted.

"Do you want to know?" she asked, bobbing on her toes.

"I do, but I'd like you to keep it a secret from me a while longer."

"Why?"

We stood there in the hall, looking at each other.

"You're going to be brilliant in New York," she said.

And once again, as always, I knew she was right.

LEAVE A REVIEW

Did you enjoy this book? You can make a big difference!

Honest reviews of my books help bring those books to the attention of other readers. If you've enjoyed this book, I would be very grateful if you could spend five minutes leaving a review (as short as you like) on the book's Amazon page.

Thank you for reading and reviewing!

ACKNOWLEDGMENTS

This project would never have come together without the encouragement and insights of a wonderful team of people:

To Amy Blair, Joanna Buck, Sarah Reuning, Corey Stewart Hassman, and Laura Weatherly: Thanks for reading early drafts of the manuscript and telling me where I was going wrong. Jane would be the target of an FBI manhunt for stalking if it weren't for you. Thanks especially to Jen Rogers, whose insightful comments and keen eye for detail ensured my manuscript made sense. Thanks also to Paula Martinac for helping me see the big picture.

To Cécile Metzger, for her exquisite cover illustration and Asya Blue, for the cover design.

To Barb Goffman and Ashley Strosnider for their copy-editing and proofreading expertise. The book is infinitely better for your time and attention.

To Laura, for her encouragement. To Paula, Corey, and

April, for cheering me on. For Barbara and Jeff, who didn't mean to encourage me but inadvertently did.

To Fred, who said, "Why the hell not?"

To Eleanor and Thomas, who create.

And most of all to Mark, who never reads before he is asked, who gives me time and space to create, and who, anytime it counts, is always on my page. I love you.

GET A SNEAK PEEK INTO HELEN'S CREATIVE PROCESS

I love to build relationships with my readers. Occasionally I send a newsletter with updates about my latest project or fun giveaways I think you might enjoy. If you sign up for my Readers' Group, I'll send you a free e-book of Jane Desmond's character profile, my main tool for creating the heroine you just met. This e-book is exclusive to my mailing list. You can't get it anywhere else.

Get it for free by signing up for the Readers' Group at https://itshelendarling.com/character-profile/

CPSIA information can be obtained
at www.ICGtesting.com
Printed in the USA
LVHW030832031118
595846LV00001B/340